THE MAID AND THE MANSION:

A MISSING GUEST

(The Maid and the Mansion Cozy Mystery—Book Three)

FIONA GRACE

Fiona Grace

Fiona Grace is author of the LACEY DOYLE COZY MYSTERY series, comprising nine books; of the TUSCAN VINEYARD COZY MYSTERY series, comprising seven books; of the DUBIOUS WITCH COZY MYSTERY series, comprising three books; of the BEACHFRONT BAKERY COZY MYSTERY series, comprising six books; of the CATS AND DOGS COZY MYSTERY series, comprising nine books; of the ELIZA MONTAGU COZY MYSTERY series, comprising nine books (and counting); of the ENDLESS HARBOR ROMANTIC COMEDY series, comprising nine books (and counting); of the INN AT DUNE ISLAND ROMANTIC COMEDY series, comprising five books (and counting); of the INN BY THE SEA ROMANTIC COMEDY series, comprising five books (and counting); and of the MAID AND THE MANSION COZY MYSTERY series, comprising five books (and counting).

Fiona would love to hear from you, so please visit www.fionagraceauthor.com to receive free ebooks, hear the latest news, and stay in touch.

ISBN: 978-1-0943-8393-4

BOOKS BY FIONA GRACE

THE MAID AND THE MANSION COZY MYSTERY
A MYSTERIOUS MURDER (Book #1)
A SCANDALOUS DEATH (Book #2)
A MISSING GUEST (Book #3)
AN UNSOLVABLE CRIME (Book #4)
AN IMPOSSIBLE HEIST (Book #5)

INN BY THE SEA ROMANTIC COMEDY
A NEW LOVE (Book #1)
A NEW CHANCE (Book #2)
A NEW HOME (Book #3)
A NEW LIFE (Book #4)
A NEW ME (Book #5)

THE INN AT DUNE ISLAND ROMANTIC COMEDY
A CHANCE LOVE (Book #1)
A CHANCE FALL (Book #2)
A CHANCE ROMANCE (Book #3)
A CHANCE CHRISTMAS (Book #4)
A CHANCE ENGAGEMENT (Book #5)

ENDLESS HARBOR ROMANTIC COMEDY
ALWAYS, WITH YOU (Book #1)
ALWAYS, FOREVER (Book #2)
ALWAYS, PLUS ONE (Book #3)
ALWAYS, TOGETHER (Book #4)
ALWAYS, LIKE THIS (Book #5)
ALWAYS, FATED (Book #6)
ALWAYS, FOR LOVE (Book #7)
ALWAYS, JUST US (Book #8)
ALWAYS, IN LOVE (Book #9)

ELIZA MONTAGU COZY MYSTERY
MURDER AT THE HEDGEROW (Book #1)
A DALLOP OF DEATH (Book #2)

CALAMITY AT THE BALL (Book #3)
A SPEAKEASY DEMISE (Book #4)
A FLAPPER FATALITY (Book #5)
BUMPED BY A DAME (Book #6)
A DOLL'S DEBACLE (Book #7)
A FELLA'S RUIN (Book #8)
A GAL'S OFFING (Book #9)

LACEY DOYLE COZY MYSTERY
MURDER IN THE MANOR (Book#1)
DEATH AND A DOG (Book #2)
CRIME IN THE CAFE (Book #3)
VEXED ON A VISIT (Book #4)
KILLED WITH A KISS (Book #5)
PERISHED BY A PAINTING (Book #6)
SILENCED BY A SPELL (Book #7)
FRAMED BY A FORGERY (Book #8)
CATASTROPHE IN A CLOISTER (Book #9)

TUSCAN VINEYARD COZY MYSTERY
AGED FOR MURDER (Book #1)
AGED FOR DEATH (Book #2)
AGED FOR MAYHEM (Book #3)
AGED FOR SEDUCTION (Book #4)
AGED FOR VENGEANCE (Book #5)
AGED FOR ACRIMONY (Book #6)
AGED FOR MALICE (Book #7)

DUBIOUS WITCH COZY MYSTERY
SKEPTIC IN SALEM: AN EPISODE OF MURDER (Book #1)
SKEPTIC IN SALEM: AN EPISODE OF CRIME (Book #2)
SKEPTIC IN SALEM: AN EPISODE OF DEATH (Book #3)

BEACHFRONT BAKERY COZY MYSTERY
BEACHFRONT BAKERY: A KILLER CUPCAKE (Book #1)
BEACHFRONT BAKERY: A MURDEROUS MACARON (Book #2)
BEACHFRONT BAKERY: A PERILOUS CAKE POP (Book #3)
BEACHFRONT BAKERY: A DEADLY DANISH (Book #4)
BEACHFRONT BAKERY: A TREACHEROUS TART (Book #5)
BEACHFRONT BAKERY: A CALAMITOUS COOKIE (Book #6)

CHAPTER ONE

Croissants, Mary Adams decided, were truly a labor of love.

She'd had the opportunity to savor these flaky, buttery, crispy delicacies quite a few times since moving away from Stoke-on-Trent after losing her factory job when the men returned from the war. It was an enjoyable perk of her new career as a housemaid, working in stately homes.

But not until now that she was helping full time in the kitchens of Drakeley Castle, had she realized exactly how much effort went into their making. It took days!

It all began with mixing and rolling the large bowl of dough out on the large steel kitchen counter. Then the dough was set aside to prove – usually overnight. Then it was time to add the layer of butter – thick and pale yellow-gold, exactly the same color as her hair, which was firmly tied back in a ponytail, and covered in a chef's hat during her working hours.

With the butter added, it was time for rolling again. Then, time to put the dough away to chill. Then, more rolling and folding and rolling and folding – until her arms ached from wielding the rolling pin, in exactly the way they'd ached in the days she'd been on the assembly line in the machinery factory.

Mary liked the feeling of tired arms, because she associated it with good, hard work. It was all part of the security of having a job, which in today's world, was all-important – especially when you were alone in the world, like she was.

Finally, after what felt like hours of folding and rolling, the croissants were ready for cutting, shaping and baking. That was the stage she was at now. The dough had been perfectly rolled and meticulously prepared – at any rate, she hoped so. Now at last, it was time to cut it into the small triangles that, when baked, would puff and crisp up into something so delicious it was nothing short of miraculous.

Checking the clock on the kitchen wall, Mary saw it was seven-thirty a.m.

"Those are looking good," the cook, Mrs. Waddington, praised. "Little beauties."

1

"Thank you," she said. "I hope I'm getting the knack for them."

This is what – your fourth try at 'em?"

Croissants were made on a Friday, Saturday and Sunday morning from the same batch of dough. Since Mary had been here a month – the cook was right. This was her fourth try at the dough, and it was the closest to perfection she'd gotten so far.

"It is," she agreed.

"Better and better each time," Mrs. Waddington said, and Mary glowed inwardly at her kindness and positive words. What a difference it made to be in an encouraging environment.

"But make sure about those sizes, eh?" the cook added, a note of warning in her voice. "You know how particular the duchess is that things get done right, especially with this big event coming up. We don't want you getting on the wrong side of her."

"I'll make sure," Mary said, focusing anew on her accuracy. It would be awful to disappoint the duchess, or the guests, with untidy pastries of varying size.

She had to admit, it was the head staff here, the cook, housekeeper and butler, who ran a kindly and supportive work environment. She wasn't sure about the owners, Duke and Duchess Drakeley, who seemed stern, particular, and rather remote.

Still, she didn't deal directly with them, but with the cook and housekeeper.

After she and Hannah had moved here, following a – well – unfortunate incident at their last workplace, Hannah had been assigned to housemaid duties, but with the castle team a kitchen maid short, and the kitchens busy, Mary had been assigned there.

There was a lot of cleaning and basic preparation involved, tireless scrubbing of floors and washing of vegetables, and careful chopping of meat – but there was also the fun of baking, which she really enjoyed.

And best of all, the kitchen was by far the warmest place in the otherwise cold and drafty castle. The stone building was set high on a hill, which Mary could see must have been most strategic when looking out for invading enemy forces. But when it came to choosing a place protected from the brisk northerly winds that scoured their way over the hills nonstop in late winter – well, that place was not Castle Drakeley.

It stood in the teeth of the wind – a tall, narrow castle with three floors, lots of winding stairways, slotted windows, and a total of fifteen chilly bedrooms, along with a couple of parlors, a great hall, two drawing rooms, a library, a cellar, and even a tiny and long-disused underground dungeon.

The first day that Mary had worked there, when the butler, Brody, had kindly shown her and Hannah around, he'd pointed out all the main rooms and all the shortcuts between them. He had even taken them down the slippery stone stairs, as far as the narrow doorway in the stone that led to the dungeons.

"We don't use them for storage, because the damp's fearsome," Brody had said. "It would have taken a skinny prisoner to get through this doorway. I suppose they had to put the fat people somewhere else." Mary had laughed at that, and he'd curled his mouth down to suppress a smile, in a way that told her he was used to making sure his expression revealed nothing it shouldn't. "But at least," he'd added, "down there, you're out of the wind."

Mary had become used to the flapping noise of the flags that flew from the castle's turrets. They wore out very quickly, the footmen had told her. Every few months, they had to put together a precarious system of ladders and scaffolding that was the only way of accessing two of the towers, and replace the old, tattered ones with new, bright and beautiful ones.

She hoped that despite these strong wintry gales, the castle would be warm enough for the arriving guests to be comfortable, and that they would enjoy the food, which she felt personally responsible for this time.

"What's this party for?" Mary asked, placing the croissants exactly the right distance away from each other on the buttered tray, while the cook vigorously stirred a large pot of oats – with honey, cream and brown sugar, this was a family breakfast favorite.

"It's a celebration of some kind," the cook said.

"A birthday? Or some other event?" Mary felt curious now, as she opened the enormous oven and slotted the tray inside. The croissants baking would soon fill the kitchen with the most mouthwatering aroma that would flood the castle, signaling to family and guests alike that breakfast was about to be served.

Turning to the other oven and wrapping two dishcloths carefully around her hands, she removed the tray of scones. They looked perfect. Fluffy, well risen, with pale sides and lightly golden brown tops, and the sweet smell of cooked flour and light crumb.

The cook shrugged her plump shoulders. "You know what the duke and duchess are like. They only tell servants what they need to know.

But I've seen you gossiping with Diana a few times," she added with a grin. Ask her. She'll be in here any minute to get some food."

Diana was the duke and duchess's only child, who at twenty-three years old was the same age as Mary, and in the month she'd been working here, Mary had become surprisingly good friends with her.

And, when scones left the oven, Mary knew full well, Diana Drakeley would soon arrive in the kitchen.

In fact, there she was, peeking around the door.

Seeing that the cook had bustled all the way to the other side of the kitchen, directing the other maid who was making stewed fruit, Mary beckoned Diana over.

The slender, dark-haired young woman tiptoed into the kitchen.

Sneaking breakfast food had become their fun morning ritual. Mary loved it that Diana was very friendly, and unlike many of the upper classes, she didn't seem to be bothered about whether people were from highborn or humble origins.

Now, in a white tunic, a blue skirt, and a green jacket that happened to be the exact color of Mary's eyes, Diana was more smartly dressed than usual. There was definitely something afoot. Usually she'd have been in shabby old hiking pants – or even still in her pajamas.

"Good morning!" Mary greeted her with a grin. "You look nice today!"

She waited for Diana to grin in return and for them to enjoy their usual morning chat. But immediately, she saw that Diana's demeanor was thoughtful and sad.

"Thanks," she said, with more of a grimace than a smile. She was not her usual bright-eyed self, full of jokes and fun.

"What's up?" Concerned, Mary lowered her voice. She'd never known Diana to be in a bad mood. She'd always seemed to be on a remarkably even keel. In fact, Mary had admired her uniformly calm and happy disposition.

Something must have occurred to change that.

Worse still, it didn't seem as if Diana was even ready to tell her. She shook her head hard, closing her eyes briefly, and when she opened them, Mary was shocked to see tears in them.

"My life is over," she said, and the flat way she said it sent a chill down Mary's spine, because Diana was not one for exaggeration. "As from tomorrow – it's all over for me."

CHAPTER TWO

Mary was shocked by the dull, leaden tone in Diana's voice, and her hopeless demeanor. Whatever had happened to cause this, it was clearly not something that could be discussed amid the bustle and noise of the kitchen.

Thinking fast, she turned and took a plate from the shelf on the wall, whisked two warm scones off the tray and onto the plate, and gently grasped Diana's hand.

"Let's go and have some tea," she said, "and you can tell me all about it."

Her next job was to take the croissants out of the oven. With a twenty-minute bake time, that a short, but hopefully adequate gap, to try to find out the problem.

Diana trailed behind her as Mary led the way to the small room adjoining the kitchen, which now did duty as a tearoom that was used by all the staff.

With the cook now involved in sweetening the stewed fruit, Mary didn't think she'd worry about a brief disappearance – as long as Mary didn't let those croissants burn.

In the tearoom, Diana slumped down onto a chair, while Mary poured two cups from the enormous pot on the shelf. It had been on the go since very early this morning, so the tea was stewed, rather than brewed, but with a dash of creamy milk and a spoon of sugar, Mary thought the cups looked just fine.

She pushed one in Diana's direction and waited for the duchess's daughter to collect her thoughts. In the meantime, she was encouraged to see that Diana broke off a tiny fragment of the steaming scone, and nibbled at it. But then she sat once more in silence. Was she going to tell Mary at all? Or would some subtle encouragement be in order?

To fortify herself, Mary took a huge bite of her scone. That dough rolling had been hard work, and having been in the kitchens since five a.m., she was starving.

As soon as she could talk without rudely spraying crumbs over the table, she set about finding out what the problem was.

"You're not normally like this," she said, "and I've never heard you speak in such a despairing way. I know it must be something serious?"

"Mary, it's beyond serious. It's a disaster that I've known will happen, but I've somehow hoped it won't." Diana nibbled at another fragment of scone, and Mary had the uneasy feeling that she wasn't even noticing the rich, delicious, crumbly mouthful. "Like I said, now it is happening, my life is over."

"Over, how?" Scenarios spun through Mary's mind. What could have caused this clearly serious situation?

She had guessed, for a while now, that the Drakeley family's fortunes were modest. The castle was rather tumbledown, and it was Mary's opinion that a lot of the rooms could do with being refurbished and renovated. Not to mention, given better protection against the cold and the damp. Was there a financial problem? Was the family going to have to sell the castle?

That was her best guess, and she knew that it would be utterly traumatic for Diana and her parents to lose their home. But as Diana started speaking, she realized she was partly right and partly wrong.

"I'm going to be married," Diana said.

She was not saying this like it was a happy event. It was the tone of voice someone might use if they had been condemned to prison in an isolation cell. Frowning in anxiety, Mary listened.

"It's a – well, it's one of those silly marriages that are organized between families when both the children are young. I've known about it – well, for most of my life. Mother always used to say, "when our union with the Barnsby-Loxtons takes place," but I never really thought, seriously, about what that meant for me."

Mary felt utterly horrified. Surely this was unacceptable in today's modern times? This was early 1947! Women should be able to choose who they married in these emancipated times! Or so Mary had always assumed. It seemed she was wrong.

"Don't you have a say in it?" she asked carefully, knowing that she was treading on ground that she didn't fully understand. She didn't want to offend Diana. A month's acquaintance that had developed into friendship was still not enough time for Mary to understand the complex pressures that the likeable young woman might be experiencing. All the same, she did think those words needed saying.

Diana shook her head. "It's been contractually agreed. You see, our family –" Here her voice dropped to a mere whisper, and Mary leaned

6

forward, eager not to miss a word that might help her understand things better.

"Our family has a very prestigious title. A dukedom is the highest level of peerage apart from the king. It's a title that other families want to acquire and marry into. Normally it would go to the male heir, but since I'm the only heir, my father consulted with his solicitors, and I will inherit it, along with whoever I marry."

"And that obviously makes it all more complicated?" Mary said, now understanding better.

"Yes. Hugh will be the next Duke of Drakeley, and in return, our family will get a share of their wealth and lands – which are considerable, and which my parents need. Things haven't been easy the past few years."

She grimaced helplessly, and Mary sat in silent sympathy, wrapping her hands tightly around her tea mug. She could now see all the complexities in the situation. Of course, Diana didn't want to disappoint her parents, but even more, she didn't want to deny them the chance to prop up their flagging fortunes with an infusion of wealth from a family keen for a top peerage title.

Mary was quite frankly puzzled by all of it. Why should titles be so sought after? Why couldn't people get by without them? Having a title, in her admittedly small experience, didn't make you a better person or a kinder person or a more worthy individual.

But then, she could see that a whole lot of rather undesirable traits, like ego and ambition, would also be in play.

"And you can't negotiate your way out of this?" she asked.

Diana shook her head. "It would have happened a couple of years ago if it hadn't been for the war. Now, it's all happening, and it's unstoppable. Tomorrow night is the engagement party, and that's going to be the start of it all. I'll be married in midsummer, but as of tomorrow, my life and my love will no longer be my own."

Mary took a sip of the warm, strong tea, hoping that it would give her a jolt of inspiration. There had to be a way out of this – didn't there?

But what if there wasn't? What if this arrangement was grinding into gear as inexorably as the huge conveyor belt at the factory where she'd worked, and there was no way of changing the future at all?

Diana must have been crying for hours. Her eyes were swollen and reddened. She must have spent a terrible night, in tears of desperation, trying to think of a way out of this dilemma, but in the end, resigning herself to the harsh reality that there wasn't one.

"Isn't there another way your family can get a bit more fortune in other ways?" she asked. "Something they can – they can sell? Treasure, jewels?" she hazarded.

But Diana shook her head sadly.

"The treasure and jewels were all sold off years ago. And we've always had a shortage of land, with only fifty acres, most of which is not suitable for farming. The Barnsby-Loxtons have millions, and their land covers several thousand acres of pristine farmland." She began to say something else, hesitated, and clamped her lips firmly shut.

Mary nodded. This Barnsby-Loxton family was sounding like a juggernaut in terms of their power, and she knew that especially in the upper classes, wealth and power gave you the ability to get what you wanted, most times.

But there was something else. Staring anxiously at Diana's trembling lower lip and her eyes, which were now welling up again with tears, she sensed that whatever this disaster was, she hadn't gotten to the bottom of it yet.

"There's more," she said, and saw Diana's eyes widen in surprise at her guess. "I think there's something you're not telling me about?"

She waited, feeling her stomach churn with tension at the desperation of Diana's predicament. And then, in a trembling voice, her friend admitted the truth.

CHAPTER THREE

"My heart belongs to someone else."

Mary's heart thudded into her shoes at Diana's whispered words This made the situation a hundred times worse.

"Who is he? Would your parents mind if you married him instead?" Mary asked. It was a reflexive question, but her brain was already racing, wondering if this person might be an acceptable last-minute substitute.

But Diana shook her head. "I can't tell you his name. And no, he wouldn't be acceptable in their eyes, because he has far less wealth. So I can't even suggest it. But, when this goes ahead – I'm going to lose my chance at happiness with him, forever." She stared at Mary through brimming eyes. "Now, do you see why all of this is so impossible? And the worst of it is – Hugh is a truly hateful man. I don't like him. I despise him. And I'd rather die than spend my life with him!"

"I'm so sorry, Diana, this is terrible." There didn't seem to be anything else for Mary to say. Even though her brain was now racing with ideas, none of them were even remotely logical or workable. I was as if poor Diana had been caught in a trap, one that had been crafted over the years and was solid and immovable and inescapable.

Imagine having to spend the rest of your life with a person you loathed and despised.

Mary's imagination couldn't even stretch that far.

There were terrible drawbacks to being in the upper classes, she now realized. At least in the working class, people could usually marry whoever they wanted. There were none of these strange rules and arrangements, where a balance of wealth and prestige was negotiated and the knot tied to seal the deal.

She would have felt exactly the same way as Diana if she'd been forced to marry a man she hated, while turning her back on somebody she loved.

"I don't think you can go ahead with this," she said firmly. "It's your life at stake, Diana. The family fortune is one thing – but your own personal happiness is another."

9

Mary knew that she was offering advice far above her station. As a humble kitchen maid, she was in no way qualified to offer this advice, but position and title aside, as a human being, she couldn't keep silent about the way she felt.

In her short experience so far, she'd met her share of unlikeable aristocrats. She'd worked for people who were insensitive, cruel, uncaring, and who valued possessions far more than they did their children or their servants.

Duke and Duchess Drakeley had their moments. The duke would often come into the kitchens to pinch some food from off a serving plate, and would joke and laugh with the maids and thank them for their work. The Duchess had personally come down to Mary's and Hannah's shared basement room on their first evening, to bring them a tin of biscuits and to see if they were settled in.

But generally speaking, despite showing a kind side, the two of them were strict, staid, and rather stuffy. And unfortunately, that attitude extended to their own daughter and her marriage wishes. She thought they would consider an arranged marriage to be 'inevitable', something that shouldn't be questioned.

"You should speak to your mother," Mary urged. "If you don't say something, then they'll never know."

But Diana shook her head. "I can't speak to them now. It's all far too late." She counted off on her fingers. "On the announcement of the engagement – which is tomorrow night – a hundred acres of land passes to our family, on a section of land they own that borders ours. Then on the marriage day, the title passes to Hugh, and my family gets another hundred acres of land, together with a financial settlement."

Hmmm, Mary thought. That didn't sound entirely fair to her. This family owned thousands of acres, and they were parting with only two hundred acres in the marriage deal? And in exchange for a very prestigious title? She hoped the financial settlement would make up for it.

Nothing could make up for the fact that Diana would have an unhappy life, wed to a man she despised. Even all the acres that the Barnsby-Loxtons owned couldn't atone for that level of misery.

At least, now that she'd unburdened herself, it looked as if Diana felt better – for the time being, anyway. Finally, she took a good-sized sip of her tea, although she didn't touch the remainder of her scone.

"I'm just glad to have had you to listen," she said. "I think it's helped to talk. Maybe – I don't know. Maybe it won't be as bad as I think it's going to be."

The level of hopelessness in her voice contradicted the words, but Mary was pleased that she was at least considering that it might not be as bad as it seemed.

"When's the last time you saw Hugh?" she asked.

"A few weeks ago, for a couple of short visits. We haven't spent any real time together for years," Diana admitted. "He fought in the war – he had officer status. He's been back a few months, but has traveled a lot. And tomorrow night, on our engagement evening, is the first time I'll actually sit down to a formal dinner with him, since he's been back. I'm dreading it so much."

Shaking her head, she got up and hurried out of the kitchen, leaving Mary to rush back to her croissants. She was just in time. Hearing about that predicament had taken up more time than she'd thought. Another minute and the delightful pastries would have burned. As it was they were perfectly golden brown, and smelled delicious as she swiftly drew the tray out, and set it on the countertop to cool.

A moment later, she jumped as she heard Duchess Drakeley's voice from the kitchen door.

"Good morning, ladies! How are you this morning?"

"Good, thank you, ma'am," Mary turned, bowing her head briefly in greeting.

"We have so much to prepare for, with this event taking place tomorrow night. I need to discuss things with you, Mrs. Waddington, as well as the head housekeeper. The Duke and I aren't sure about some of the menu items." She glanced at Mary doubtfully. "If you think you might have some suggestions, I suppose you can also join in."

Mary was flummoxed by how positive she sounded about this dinner. Did she have no inkling that her poor daughter was going to be embarking on a life of misery?

She guessed it hadn't even crossed the duchess's mind. And as for the secret love, who Diana wanted to marry – well, that was so secret, she hadn't even told Mary his name. So, the parents believed that in following the contractually arranged agreement, this was going to be a happy and wonderful occasion for all.

It gave Mary a sense of sadness, as she walked over to where Duchess Drakeley was opening her big leather bound notebook, to know that this wasn't the truth at all.

"We have a happy announcement to make tomorrow night," she said in excited tones, and Mary hastily pasted on a smile.

"Well now, ma'am, that's something to look forward to," the cook agreed, as the housekeeper, Miss Knott, bustled in.

"As far as menus go, I think something seasonal but festive will be best. It would be nice if we could include a touch of spring on the menu. I know it's still a few weeks away, but I'd like to give people a message of hope and happiness to come!"

Perplexed, but being careful not to show it, Mary nodded. It was becoming clearer to her that Duchess Drakeley genuinely did not have the faintest idea that anything was wrong. She was happily anticipating an event that had been planned ever since poor Diana's birth and which was now coming to fruition.

Didn't she understand that Diana loathed Hugh? Maybe not, if he'd been away fighting in the war for years. She might never realize. Or if she did, it would be too late.

"Hope and happiness," the cook said enthusiastically. "I think there are some flowers in the conservatory, for the table, and some figs and pears, too, that have grown well in that sheltered, sunny spot. So we'll be able to make something with them, I'm sure."

"The guests will start arriving this afternoon. We're expecting the guest of honor, a man called Hugh Barnsby-Loxton, and his parents." Excitement radiated from her voice. "Hugh's good friend and neighbor, Cameron Pratt, will also be there, and so will Lady Emily, who's one of Diana's school friends, and a few other friends from further afield. We'll have to try to allocate them the warmest bedrooms for this time of year – I know that's a challenge."

"A good supply of blankets and a hot water bottle will help," the housekeeper said firmly. "We'll keep the windows closed and the curtains drawn, and make sure there's adequate firewood in each room." She paused. "We should probably not use the guest room at the end of the corridor. That room is terribly drafty."

"Then let's not use it unless absolutely necessary," the duchess agreed. "However, it will be better to have all the guests on the same side of the castle, if we can. It's such a special occasion. Everyone must be comfortable."

Mary guessed that Duchess Drakeley had probably been talking, in that hopeful way, about the improvements they were going to make to the castle, and their future plans for farming – and now, Mary could see that part of Diana's dilemma was a very genuine desire to not let her parents down.

There had to be a way of solving this, Mary mused, and for a moment, she was so focused on how this could be done that she tuned all the way out of the discussion on the room allocation.

She tuned back in with a jolt when she heard a familiar name.

"And Gilbert MacLeod," the duchess said. "His parents unfortunately have a prior engagement – it's a neighbor's fiftieth birthday – so they won't be able to attend. But he responded to the invitation very promptly and said he'd love to be here."

Gilbert? He was going to be here? And better still, he'd responded to the invitation with alacrity. She felt a thrill of excitement at seeing the tall, dark haired man, with his infectious smile and those deep blue eyes, and the freckles on his nose. It felt wrong to be looking forward to an event that was going to plunge Diana into a life of sadness, but Mary couldn't help feeling a blaze of anticipation at this news.

It was also laced with trepidation, though. Things hadn't gone entirely smoothly the last time they'd met. Being caught up in a murder investigation had been a huge complication. For a while, she'd suspected Gilbert of committing the crime, and although he hadn't said anything to her at the time, she worried that it had left him feeling differently toward her.

It might change their friendship, when they met again, now that Gilbert had had some time to think about things.

"Gilbert MacLeod. He's from up north, near Scotland, isn't he?" the housekeeper asked, looking down at her bedroom list.

"Yes," Duchess Drakeley said.

"If he's from up north," the housekeeper said thoughtfully, "he might not mind one of the colder rooms."

Mary almost opened her mouth to say that Gilbert didn't like cold rooms, and had complained about how cold and drafty his family's stately home was. He'd done so in a very amusing way. It had made her grin – but had also raised questions in her mind.

And it was those questions that had led to the revelation that Gilbert, like her, was from a poor background. He hadn't been born into wealth and status. His parents had made money through a successful furniture business, and they'd only ended up with a stately home because the previous owner had begged them to buy it.

That was the only reason that Gilbert and his parents were rubbing shoulders with the upper classes today. Of course, being Gilbert, he'd started his own successful business, involving hybrid seeds, which took him around the country on visits to large estates.

She *almost* blurted out, "Oh, Gilbert's not fond of the cold!" but then realized how it would sound. It would sound incredibly forward, and as if she knew him well – which she didn't, although she wanted to know him better.

But it was too late. Both the housekeeper and Duchess Drakeley had heard her quick inhalation of breath, and probably seen the look in her eyes. Now they were waiting for her to say what she'd been going to.

She couldn't say that! So she'd better think of something else – fast.

"I was just considering the menus," she said hurriedly, "and I was wondering if a rich, creamy trout soup would work?"

The housekeeper wrinkled her nose as if she considered Mary's comment a little random and off-topic for the moment. But the cook nodded decisively.

"The soup will be a very good idea," she said. "It'll pair well with the main course I was thinking of, which is a roast beef dish, with roast potatoes, Yorkshire pudding, and some peas and carrots. Simple and traditional, but definitely one to please the majority of the guests – some of whose preferences we don't yet know."

"Yes, it'll be important to make sure everyone likes the menu, and I know that Hugh and Cameron are not fans of anything too exotic or adventurous," Duchess Drakeley said. "Hugh always says that fighting in the war changed his tastes, and that he'd live on officer's rations if he could."

Mary pasted on a smile and nodded in an interested way. Hugh didn't sound like a bad person. Liking simple food was not a character flaw, and she personally thought it could be an advantage.

Maybe a miracle would happen, and at this dinner party, Diana would forget about her nameless love interest, and she'd fall head over heels for the man she was supposed to marry.

But, if she seemed in the least doubtful or upset – then what was Mary going to do?

She'd need to have a plan to save the day. And as she puzzled over it while the cook wrote her lists, a workable, though risky, idea was beginning to dawn in her mind.

CHAPTER FOUR

As soon as it was time for her lunch break, she hurried in search of Hannah, so that she could update her on the very serious crisis that was unfolding at Drakeley Castle.

Hannah, with the team of three other housemaids, was busily preparing the least drafty of the bedrooms, ready for the arrival of the small group of guests.

Rushing up to the second-last room in the corridor, Mary found her friend shaking out a sheet, before smoothing it down on the four-poster bed that stood near the narrow window.

"Mary! Is it lunchtime already?" Hannah's curls were not entirely covered by the uniform cap. Her rich brown hair bobbed and bounced around her face as she tugged the sheet into place.

Going to the bottom of the bed, Mary helped her with the next sheet, and with the array of blankets that would hopefully ensure a comfortable night's sleep for the occupant of this room.

Castles, as Mary had discovered since working here, were inherently older, and colder, than the manor houses she'd known. Perhaps in the height of summer, this room would be delightfully cool – but that felt like a very long way away.

"I've got an issue to discuss with you," Mary said, and Hannah's eyes widened.

"What is it?" she said anxiously.

Mary grasped the edge of the woolen blanket, surprisingly soft and warm, pulled it down, and tucked it into place.

She was glad that she had such a close and trustworthy friend working with her. Hannah's friendship, and her fun personality, meant the world to Mary. And even though they didn't see much of each other during their busy workdays, at least they shared a room, and could catch up on gossip and news in whispers, before falling asleep in their small basement hideaway at the back of the castle.

"It's Diana," Mary said in a low voice.

"What's wrong with Diana?" Hannah's voice resonated with puzzlement. Mary knew she'd also noticed how even-tempered and happy Diana was. It made this a right shock, she thought.

15

"She's being forced to marry someone she doesn't like – in fact, someone she hates," Mary said. "That's what this event tomorrow night is all about. It's the announcement of their engagement."

Hannah froze, momentarily forgetting about the next blanket.

"How can they force Diana to marry somebody?" she asked, the same reasonable question that Mary had first thought of.

"It's because there's an arrangement in place, going back years, involving money, and family alliances, and a title." Mary hoped this summary would suffice, because although she entrusted Hannah to keep any and all secrets, she also didn't want to give every single detail away that she'd learned.

But Hannah rolled her eyes.

"Oh, that again?" she said resignedly. "At one of the other houses where I worked, there was the same problem. The man had the title, the woman had the wealth. They were the most unhappy couple I've ever known. I honestly think the only happy people were the parents."

"Well, the problem is that the Duke and Duchess don't know how Diana feels," Mary said. "She won't tell them. I think it's a case of not wanting to upset them, because she loves them, and they – er – they need the money," she added in a whisper.

This really felt like giving too much away, but luckily, it was nothing that Hannah didn't already know.

"Gossip in my team of housemaids is that they're on the brink of going bankrupt. They desperately need more farmland, apparently," she said. "With a good few acres put to crops, and some room for a big flock of sheep, it could turn things around for them."

Mary nodded. Housemaids, it seemed, were very well tuned into a family's situation. And she could now see how those two lots of hundred acres would both prove so vital. Presumably, the deal specified that they were good farmland.

But at what cost?

"I've been trying to think how we can help."

"Help? Us?" Hannah sounded dubious. "Isn't that way outside our scope? We could get into trouble."

"I know we shouldn't, and that it's wrong for maids to even think of interfering in these affairs – but it's Diana's future happiness at stake." she said, getting to work on the next blanket now that Hannah's moment of frozen surprise was over.

"And? Don't tell me you've come up with a solution?" Hannah quirked an eyebrow.

"I've been thinking of one that might work," Mary said. "You see, if this Hugh character is really as obnoxious and dislikeable as he seems to be, we need to make him show his true colors. Because if the parents see that, then surely they will realize they can't condemn poor Diana to a life of misery?"

Hannah thought about that, as they put the third and final blanket on the bed, turned the top of the sheet down, and then shook out the counterpane, which was a sky blue, with ivory embroidery all over it in an intricate pattern of flowers and leaves.

"You're saying, we create a situation where that will happen?" Hannah asked, placing the blue and ivory cushions on the bed.

"Yes. We need to force his hand and show the whole group of guests what he's like," Mary said confidently.

"And how are we going to do that?"

She was so glad that Hannah was saying 'we', and that her loyal and adventurous friend was up for this. That was a big positive.

Unfortunately, there was also a big negative, and that was that Mary had not yet thought of any way to do it.

"That's what I wanted to discuss with you. I mean, I've come up with the concept," she reiterated hopefully. "But the details do need filling in."

Hannah picked up the empty laundry basket. "In that case, let's talk about it over some lunch," she said.

They hurried downstairs, passing along the draftiest of the corridors, that had an actual breeze blowing down it when the wind gusted from the northwest – which was just about all the time in winter.

Mary didn't know much about building costs, but she suspected insulating the corridor against the cold would be an extremely expensive exercise. And this was just one corridor, in a medium sized, but highly porous and chilly, castle.

Having gone down the breezy, chilly passage, they swung right, and headed into the kitchen through the scullery entrance, going straight to the staff tearoom.

There was a plate of sandwiches on the table, fresh and delicious. There was only one hot meal for the staff, and that was a generous high tea, but scones, snacks and sandwiches were available throughout the day, as well as cups of vegetable broth, tasty and warming.

The sandwiches today consisted of egg mayonnaise, ham, and a chicken liver pate that had been on the dinner menu the day before. Mary was delighted to try it. She'd played her part in mixing that pate for what had seemed like hours, while adding masses of butter, to get the creamy, rich consistency. Now to taste it.

They loaded their plates with sandwiches, and then headed back to the corner of the tearoom, to eat their lunch standing up, while hungry butlers, maids and stable hands came in to grab some food.

"I think a key point," Mary said thoughtfully, "is how unpleasant people treat others, when they are in a difficult situation, and when those people can't do anything for them."

"Yes," Hannah said, "that definitely shows off their character. But my problem is this."

"Your problem is what?" Mary frowned. Wasn't her idea going to be workable?

"My problem is that these obnoxious people who are so dislikeable, often pretend they're different, and good, in front of others. And if he's that person, then he'll behave like a hero in front of everyone. Only when he's alone will he show his true colors," she said wisely.

Mary sighed. That was a stumbling block. It would be utterly pointless to get Hugh Barnsby-Loxton alone and then get him to show who he really was, when there was nobody around to see.

"Also," Hannah said, deflating Mary's plans still further, "what if he's not really a bad person? He might just not be suited to Diana."

And again, Mary had to admit, there was wisdom in her friend's words. Especially since she hadn't told Hannah that Diana loved somebody else. Maybe that love for this mystery man, was prejudicing her against Hugh, and he was in fact a likeable person whose only character failing was not being the mystery man.

"It's not as simple as I thought it would be," she said.

"Don't worry," Hannah said. "It's better to try to think of everything that could go wrong beforehand than when your plan's in action, isn't it?"

And that was the truth. Mary gave her a conspiratorial nod.

"Let's work on it all the same," she agreed. "And perhaps part one of the plan, the most important part, needs to be assessing Hugh as soon as he arrives." She lowered her voice. "The way he treats us, when nobody's watching, will tell us a lot about him. And we can do that by putting him to the test – our test."

CHAPTER FIVE

How frustrating it was, Mary thought, pacing up and down in the hallway the following day, that plans never turned out the way you wanted them to? She'd hoped that Hugh Barnsby-Loxton would be one of the earliest arrivals. He was, after all, coming to announce his betrothal and spend time with his new fiancée.

She'd banked on this, and on having a good few hours to interact with him and get a sense of what kind of person he was – and if he was nasty and unpleasant, to think about what kind of plan would expose him.

But just an hour ago, at ten a.m., the message had come through that the Barnsby-Loxtons were delayed, thanks to the surprise arrival of a few visitors.

Mary had heard Duchess Drakeley's voice resounding from out of the parlor where the telephone was.

"Please, bring them along if you like! The more, the merrier!" There had been a note of panic in her voice, though, because now all the warmer bedrooms were in use.

But as she hovered outside the parlor, picking up on the one-sided conversation, Mary had concluded that they were going to have a light luncheon with the visitors and then get going.

That meant right now, in this hallway, with its flagstoned floor and the rather worn red carpet, and the shield and sword mounted on the wall above the old wooden table, they were waiting for the other guests to arrive.

And then, she and the two footmen turned expectantly to the door as the first visitor approached.

From the road, a couple of hundred yards away, they saw the plume of the exhaust fumes misting in the chilly morning air. The car, a smart, serviceable, navy blue Riley RM, turned up the driveway. As it progressed, it bounced heavily over the potholes that the recent heavy rains had created, and jounced over the uneven places where the paving had been completely worn away.

Who was this, Mary wondered, narrowing her eyes against the misty, bright light as she stared at the car. There wasn't time now to look again at the guest list and confirm things.

The car stopped at the turning circle in front of the castle's main doorway. The two butlers at the door both sprang to attention, moving forward as one. Mary waited behind, standing with a few of the other maids, ready to ferry the guests' possessions in as soon as possible, and get them settled in. It was fine, now, but those fierce winds could blow clouds in at an astonishingly fast rate, and there was rain expected by lunch time.

The car door opened, and out climbed a man of average height, who looked to be in his early thirties. He had broad shoulders, a thatch of buttery blond hair, and hazel eyes. He was wearing a warm, comfortable-looking brown coat, and in his hand, he held a small posy of flowers.

Who was this? Mary's curiosity sharpened. He was bringing the hostess flowers, which was polite and kind, but who was he? She wondered all the more as the two footmen hesitated, glancing at each other before moving slowly out to meet him.

And then, Duchess Drakeley hurried through the hallway. She was wearing a smart, yet outdoorsy, tweed jacket, and a navy blue skirt. On her head, she wore a stylish waterproof hat. But on her face, as she passed, Mary picked up a worried expression.

"I'm not sure who this is," she heard her mutter, and Mary's eyes widened.

A mystery guest?

Watching, fascinated, Mary edged forward as the duchess hurried out of the door and down the five stone stairs to meet the driver.

"Good morning. I am Duchess Drakeley," she said politely, her voice resonating in the quiet morning. "May I ask your name, sir?"

"Lucas Everington," he said. He fixed her with a clear, bold gaze. "I'm passing by here, and wanted to stop in on personal business. However, I can see this might not be a good time. Are you expecting other guests?"

From his voice, Mary didn't think that Lucas was one of the upper classes, although he was well spoken, and from his car, and his clothing, and his jacket, he was definitely wealthy. He was a total mystery person, though, and she wondered what the purpose of his visit here was.

Was it really a coincidence that he was here at the same time as the engagement party? Or was it an honest coincidence - after all, it was a Friday, and a good day for traveling out of town, or to a faraway place.

Duchess Drakeley drew herself up, and Mary sensed an internal battle was taking place. For a few moments, she simply stood. And then, in a gracious voice, she said, "We are delighted to welcome you to Drakeley Castle, Mr. Everington. Have you traveled far?"

"From two counties over," he said, gesturing to the south. "I've been on the road since early this morning."

"Well, you are most welcome to find hospitality with us," the duchess said. "We will require some time to make you up a room, should you wish to stay overnight?"

"If you are busy preparing, I don't wish to take your valuable time," he said apologetically. "I can always come back tomorrow?"

"But you have had a long drive," Duchess Drakeley said, manners taking precedence once more. "We do have a family event this evening with a number of invited guests. You are most welcome to join us, and to speak to myself and my husband tomorrow about your business."

"I'm very grateful for your consideration. And your hospitality."

Duchess Drakeley beckoned over one of the butlers.

"Unpack the car, and escort this guest to the parlor. We can make up the room..." she paused, breathing deeply, "at the end of the corridor."

The one with the worst drafts? Oh, no, Mary thought. But then again, it was in the same wing as the other guests, so he wouldn't be isolated in a completely different part of the castle.

But who was this person, and why was he here?

She hoped it wasn't some kind of trouble. Given the fact that the duke and duchess were not in good financial circumstances, Mary felt worried.

Some people sensed vulnerability, that she'd learned. And he'd clearly chosen to stay the night. If he had something quick to say, he would surely have said it and been on his way. It seemed to Mary that he'd been very swift to accept the invitation to stay. It was almost as if he had been hinting at it. Almost as if he needed some time here to look around and find things out. Even now, striding through the front door, he was already looking around, glancing up at the ceiling, taking a look at the hall table, and resting his gaze, for a curious few moments, on Mary herself.

She returned it with as confident a stare as she could.

"Good morning, sir," she said politely, getting a nod in response before he moved on.

If the vultures were already circling, it might be catastrophic for her to try to prevent this marriage. What if the marriage was the only thing that could save Drakeley Castle? And what if she and Hannah conspired to do something that would end up plunging the family into ruin?

Mary knew she would have to be very careful now, or her well-meaning actions might have disastrous consequences.

CHAPTER SIX

After the strange Lucas Everington had arrived, two other guests drove up in quick succession, leaving the maids with a flurry of lifting, carrying and unpacking to do. Every time she saw a car approach, Mary felt a surge of hope that it would be the Bentley she now knew so well, and that Gilbert would arrive. She was looking forward to seeing him again so much that it was making her nervous something would go wrong.

She wanted to get it over and done with, and have him here, rather than waiting with this tight knot of expectation in her stomach.

As she was packing away the two large suitcases that the second guest had brought, she saw a shadow at the bedroom door, and glanced up.

There was Diana. She was looking as tense as Mary felt. Mary guessed that she, too, was just wanting this to be over, and that the dread she was feeling was the worst part of it.

Mary put on a cheerful face as Diana walked in.

"How are you feeling?" she asked.

In a soft voice, Diana replied, "I've been looking for you. I feel like some friendly company. I don't even like that school friend my parents invited. Can I help with this unpacking?"

"Of course you can help," she said.

"I don't feel like socializing," Diana admitted, rummaging in the suitcase and removing a pile of brightly colored briefs. "Goodness!" she said. "This is rather cheerful!"

Now that she'd found something to occupy her attention, and take her mind off the inevitable, Mary could see her quirky sense of humor was resurfacing.

"They are definitely bright and bold," she agreed.

She watched carefully as Diana put them away. If she didn't do it tidily enough, Mary would have to come back and redo the drawer at a later stage.

"You know, I wish I could run away and work in a factory, like you did," she said, folding the green, yellow and plaid briefs one by one.

"Well, you'd have a bit of a problem doing that," Mary said with a grin. "Because they're overrun with men taking the jobs all us women held down during the war."

"I know. You told me that, and I think it's so – so unfair, but yet so fascinating. I've never been in a factory. I've traveled to a few places, but really, I've had such an unadventurous life compared to you."

To Mary's relief, because the underwear hadn't been very well folded, Diana gave up on the task of unpacking and sat down on the bed, looking thoughtful.

She loved hearing the tales of Mary's factory work. Mary guessed that was because it was so far outside the scope of her own experience, it was like getting the chance to live a different life.

"I wouldn't call it adventurous. I just did what I had to do," she said, thinking sadly of her mother's final days in the hospital. Mary had been only eighteen when she'd died, and had been forced to go out and fend for herself in a world that she had soon realized was mostly harsh, though occasionally kind.

"It was really hard at first, getting used to the work," she said, as Diana folded her hands and listened, looking more calm and contented than Mary had seen her so far today. "The blisters I got at first were just terrible. And finishing each day with a thick coating of oil on my hands – really heavy, tarry, dark machine oil – that was something new. It took quite a technique to learn how to get it off. Very hot water was the key," she remembered.

"But blisters and hot water?" Diana questioned. "That must have been sore."

"It was," Mary remembered. "It was very sore. But after a while, my hands toughened up. Although it was also pretty hard on the feet, standing by that belt all day. It's funny how cold you get, just standing."

"I can imagine," Diana said, now intent on Mary's story, as if she was there, in that large, drafty factory, with its smell of oil, and the acrid fumes from the metalwork, and the constant clanging and shouting that after a while, became background noise you didn't even notice.

"So we'd stand, shivering in place, waiting for that belt to start up," Mary said, coincidentally taking three leather belts out of the suitcase as she said the word. Rolling them neatly, she placed them in a drawer. "And then, when it started, it was all action stations like there was a race on. You had to dive into that work. Those bolts were so stiff, and it was so hard to get them in place even with the oil, but they had to go on and then they had to get tightened, really tight. Tight enough that even a whole lot of bouncing and juddering over rough ground wouldn't make them come loose. Mr. Watson always used to remind us that quality standards were what kept his business alive, and quality complaints could kill a business."

"So you learned about business as well?"

"Well, not proper studies," Mary clarified, closing the suitcase and putting it neatly in the wardrobe before opening the next one. A stack of silk shirts called for careful unpacking and neat hanging in the wardrobe. "It was more like nuggets of information that he'd toss to us from time to time. They were interesting, though."

"And did you get food there?"

"Oh, no," Mary explained. "It was a work environment. We were lucky to get a cup of tea on our breaks."

"Tell me about the cups the tea came in?" It was the little details that fascinated Diana. At Castle Drakeley, the tea was served in bone china teacups – to the family, at least. The staff got theirs in the older, chipped cups and a few bigger mugs.

"The tea was served in big, white mugs. It was almost impossible to break one of them – they were very tough," Mary remembered. "And a full mug was about triple the amount of tea that you get here in these pretty cups at the castle. But they were stained inside from years and years of having tea in them. So instead of being white, they were a brownish color near the bottom."

"Goodness me," Diana said, her eyebrows quirking.

"Cups with a history – just like yours," Mary said, remembering that the bone china cups probably hailed from an earlier era and were valuable antiques. "Only a different history. A more rough and ready one."

"It's so fascinating to hear these details," Diana said.

Mary had now finished unpacking the second suitcase and placed it in the large wardrobe next to the first one.

"Well, that's done," she said. "I wonder if any other guests have arrived?"

"I'd better go down to be with my parents," Diana said reluctantly. "They'll be expecting us all to welcome the guests – and the Barnsby-Loxtons, as a family."

Her demeanor was now subdued all over again as the reality of her circumstances rushed back after the escapism of hearing about the factory labor.

She and Diana left, turning in different directions. Diana headed to the parlor while Mary went in the direction of the stairs leading down to the hallway.

But, as Mary neared the stairs, she heard a familiar voice coming from the hallway.

"Well, I'm thrilled to be here for this occasion. So good to be back, and the place is looking very shipshape!"

Her heart accelerated, hard.

It was Gilbert. He'd arrived, and this would be her chance to meet him. If she was fast, she could get to the hallway while he was still walking in.

Breathless at the thought of this reunion, she hurried to the stairs.

But, as she reached the first floor, she nearly bumped into the housekeeper. Miss Knott was looking stressed.

"Ah, Mary. Please will you go to Mr. Everington's room immediately. He's the guest who arrived unexpectedly. I'm not sure if there's a problem or if he spoke to you earlier?" Her expression was dubious as she regarded Mary. "He's just buzzed for some urgent help – and he asked for the maid who'd been in the hallway when he arrived. That was you."

CHAPTER SEVEN

Could the timing possibly be worse, Mary thought in consternation. Gilbert was literally around the corner, and now she'd been whisked away on a very strange-sounding errand.

She'd seen that Lucas Everington had noticed her when he'd arrived. His gaze had focused on her, and he had taken a good, thorough look at her.

But he didn't know her from a bar of soap, as the girls at the factory had liked to say. Why on earth was this mysterious arrival asking for her at such a time?

At any rate, instructions were instructions, and there was no arguing with them.

"I'm on my way," she said, turned around, and with an effort that took a disproportionate amount of willpower, she turned away from the hall, rushed back up the stairs, and retraced her steps along the corridor, all the way to the end.

She tapped on the door and heard a voice call, "Come in."

Mary entered to see Mr. Everington seated at the writing desk. He was busy penning a letter. She saw the neat, small, dark blue writing on the thick, plush paper, but she couldn't make out the words from where she stood.

"Ah, thanks so much for coming up here," he said in a friendly way.

"You asked for me specifically?" Mary wanted to get to the gist of why.

"Yes, I – well, seeing you were in the hallway, I thought you were helping guests out, and I didn't want to impose on anyone else's duties," he said. His tone was slightly apologetic, and the statement itself was logical.

It was just that she didn't trust it.

"Well, here I am, and how can I help?" she asked.

"I was wondering – I don't want to go down and socialize with the family because I feel I'm not a part of this gathering. But I am starving and I was hoping I could have a snack in my room?"

Mary still didn't entirely trust this reasoning, but had to admit that it now made sense, at least.

"I'll get you something immediately," she said.

"Thank you," he replied gratefully. "Er, I haven't asked, and it feels rude not to – would you mind giving me your name?"

She hesitated. The excuse of getting food might be a plausible one, but yet again she was picking up something strange in his tone now.

"Mary Adams," she replied.

"Mary Adams?" he echoed. "And have you been working here long?"

"I've been here five weeks tomorrow," she said, but her suspicions were positively bristling now. Why did he want to know this?

Maybe she should just be more trusting, Mary told herself. He could simply be trying to put her and himself at ease.

"Five weeks? And before that?"

This interest was definitely untoward, and to avoid standing here for the next hour, while he asked question after question about her life history, Mary decided it would be wisest to condense it.

"I've worked for a couple of country houses, and before that, I did a stint in a factory, filling in for the men," she said. "And now, is there anything else you need, along with the food? Some tea?"

"Tea will be good." Now that she'd managed to summarize all the answers he could possibly want, he was backing off, which she was grateful for.

"I'll fetch it now."

She turned and headed out, glad to be away from this man, whom she considered to be increasingly strange, and his odd questions.

Heading downstairs, she went to the kitchen and organized a tray with a teapot, one of the china cups, milk and sugar. She quickly checked the cold room to see what prepared food and snacks were available. On the plate, she arranged a selection of cold chipolata sausages, ham and cress sandwiches, a serving of bean salad, and a slice of fruitcake. That was hopefully tasty and filling enough to tide him over until he joined the family for pre-dinner drinks.

Arranging everything on the tray, she hurried in the direction of the stairs once more, hoping that this would be a brief encounter and that she'd just be able to put the food in the room, and go.

As she reached the stairs, footsteps were coming down.

First she heard them, quick and light. Then she saw a pair of shiny black shoes and gray trousers.

And then, looking up with her heart thudding hard, she saw a pair of broad shoulders, and a head of tousled dark hair, and that familiar, blue eyed, freckle cheeked, and undeniably handsome face.

"Mary!" Gilbert MacLeod said. "How good to see you again."

Mary had a brief moment of agonizing. She knew that in the country house environment, with rules of protocol respected, she should call him Mr. MacLeod.

But the last time she saw him, she had made a very deliberate decision that, in view of everything they'd been through, she was going to call him by his first name. She'd done so once, but now, opening her mouth, Mary lost her nerve.

"Gil – Mr. MacLeod," she stammered out. "How good to see you."

He quirked an eyebrow. "I hope it is good. Last time we met, I have a nasty feeling you suspected me of murder for a while."

Mary sighed, being careful not to wobble the tray as she did so.

"For a while, circumstances did point in that direction," she admitted.

"Investigating without fear or favor? There's a lot to be said for that." His tone was wry, and she couldn't quite figure out whether he was annoyed by what had happened, or amused by it. She felt briefly unsure.

Had this damaged their friendship?

But then, he spoke again, in a warmer tone. "I'm teasing. It was an experience I'll never forget. And going through it with you – well, that made it even more unforgettable."

"Please will you thank your mother again for organizing this job."

After she and Hannah had left their previous employment, thanks to the trouble, Gilbert's mother had kindly advised him that there was a job opportunity here, if they should need it. Mary felt beyond grateful for the immense thoughtfulness of a woman she'd never met. No wonder Gilbert was so kind. He'd been brought up that way.

"I'm so glad she was able to help. She was thrilled, too," Gilbert admitted. "She doesn't know the Drakeleys very well, but they said they might use her when they renovate their ballroom, so she's keen to foster a better friendship."

"It was so very kind of her, and an absolute lifesaver. I'm enjoying it here," she said – and she was, even though she now saw that there were too few maids and butlers for the amount of work there was to do.

"I'll pass that on to her, and I know she'll be thrilled it's going well. But, talking of work, I don't want to keep you," he added. "Well, actually, I'd love to stand and talk to you but that tray looks heavy, and the Drakeleys are waiting in the parlor to have a cup of tea with me – but hopefully, there'll be time for more conversation later?"

Now he was the one who sounded anxious, as if he was worried his teasing about the suspected murder had hit the wrong note and that now she was offended.

"Later, I'm sure there will be time. And I'm looking forward to it."

As she climbed the stairs, she felt more lighthearted than she'd done all day. Gilbert was here, they'd spoken, and things between them were good. That made the day seem brighter, even though it was actually clouding over fast, and the rain looked set to start at any moment.

She tapped on the door and opened it, balancing the tray one-handed with the ease of practice as she did so, and then brought it inside. Since Mr. Everington was still busy penning his letter at the desk, with an air of focus, she put the tray down on the small antique table next to the armchair.

"If there's anything else you need, please come down to the kitchen, and I'll assist," she said politely.

"Thank you," he said, sounding grateful, with that odd tone gone from his voice.

And then she skedaddled out of the room before he could start asking her any more strange questions.

She headed straight back down the stairs, intending to go to the kitchens and start helping with the now-frantic food preparation, but as she passed the hallway, she picked up a bustle of excitement coming from outside.

Hannah burst in through the front door, carrying a large top hat and a pair of shiny black shoes.

"He's here!" she hissed to Mary.

"Who?" she replied, confused. There weren't supposed to be any more guests arriving this morning.

"Hugh Barnsby-Loxton. He didn't wait for his parents. He drove here with his friend, Cameron Pratt, and they're both outside!"

Time to meet Diana's nemesis? As quick as she could, Mary darted out of the door.

CHAPTER EIGHT

Before Mary had even reached the threshold, she heard booming voices from outside.

"The old place is looking rather sorry for itself, isn't it?" That disparaging comment was accompanied by a braying laugh. "Seems like it would have done it a favor to be shelled in the war!"

Mary felt horrified by that completely insensitive comment as she hurried out, almost colliding with a footman on his way in, carrying a large suitcase.

Two men, both seemingly oblivious to the rain, were standing by a bright blue Jaguar. They were both tall, but the man with his back turned, was lean and fair haired, and the man facing her had broad shoulders, a bulky jaw, and a bristly, but well cut, head of dark brown hair. His eyebrows were thick and heavy, and his eyes were a piercing blue.

He was the speaker, she saw. He was the one who'd hoped for the poor castle to be shelled. He had an air of immense confidence.

Say it like it is, Mary, she told herself firmly. That, right there, is not confidence, but arrogance!"

"Guess we'd better get inside," the blond-haired man said. His voice was more refined and cooler, though still haughty.

"Oh, come on, Cameron. We were in worse rain than this when we went on our mission into Normandy, weren't we? The one where I saved the nation and won us the war?"

"My jacket's getting wet, old boy. Let's head in," Cameron said.

Both the men walked inside, without a flicker of a glance at Mary, and without taking any of their possessions out of the car. It was as if they'd just abandoned it.

She scurried through the rain, picking up an overcoat, and a plaid scarf, and a small haversack. The overcoat was already getting wet, so she hustled with her armful of clothing, getting to the shelter of the hallway as quickly as she could.

To her surprise, the two men were still there.

"That painting, there," Hugh said, gesturing to the rather dark oil painting on the far wall, of a man, with his head bowed, sitting with a

31

solemn looking greyhound by his side. "That's the one I kept telling them they needed to restore. It's too far gone now. Carelessness, that's what it is."

"It's a shame when people don't appreciate their heritage," Cameron agreed. "Strikes me they're battling for money."

"Well, we're throwing them a bone or two in the contract," Hugh said with a chuckle. "But some people have titles wasted on them."

"Come on, old boy. The family will be waiting for us in the parlor. Might as well get the boring greetings over with."

"Must ask them if they have any available horses for the weekend," Hugh muttered, turning and striding along with his friend. "Weather's supposed to clear tomorrow, but I'm doubtful of the quality of their horseflesh these days. Might have to go for a trot out on whatever old nag they have available. Or else, perhaps a neighbor can help out with something more quality."

The two men disappeared down the corridor, to Mary's relief.

She stared after them, feeling shocked by what she'd heard. Her test was unnecessary now, because this short conversation had been the eye-opener she needed. They were obnoxious and, in fact, insufferable. The two of them, Hugh in particular, seemed to have nothing but contempt for Drakeley Castle and its owners. Cameron, though a snob, had been playing along.

And most concerningly, Mary worried, as she climbed the stairs, she hadn't heard Hugh say a word about his wife-to-be. He hadn't mentioned that he was looking forward to spending time with her. *Would* he even be spending time with her? Or was the trot out on the old nag going to take priority over Diana?

Fuming now, Mary marched along the corridor to Hugh's room. She was guessing this enormous jacket belonged to him, as he was wider in the shoulders than Cameron.

Hannah was inside, finishing up with the unpacking, and Mary made sure to close the door before delivering the bad news.

"First impressions, I don't like Hugh Barnsby-Loxton at all," she whispered.

Hannah nodded grimly. "Nor do I," she whispered back. "He's an inconsiderate snob. You didn't see him earlier when I went out. He knew I was trying to unpack the car, but he didn't even move aside. He watched while I opened the back door and crawled in and started clawing at the stuff in the front, to get it out. I think he might even have laughed at me. At any rate, he muttered something about maids and their backsides getting in the way, to his blond friend. I found it very demeaning."

"That's not just inconsiderate, it's actively cruel. If you do that, you're the kind of person who enjoys the power you have over others," Mary agreed. "He was talking in such an insulting way about the castle. He has no respect for it. If it was up to him, I'm sure he'd just flatten the place."

Hannah sighed. "I don't know what to do about this. I feel so badly for Diana. But Mary, how can we stop this? It's really clear they do need the money, they do need this marriage to happen."

"We have to stop it somehow," Mary insisted.

"And if the Drakeleys lose their castle?"

"They won't lose it, I'm sure," she said, but she could hear the doubt in her own tone. She wasn't privy to their finances. Their situation could be even more precarious than she thought it was. Diana could be sacrificing her happiness for what she believed to be the best possible cause.

At that moment, a rap on the door made them both jump guiltily.

Mary rushed over and opened it to find herself staring at a lean, slight man with fine features and immaculately cut dark hair. He was wearing a black jacket that was smart but cheap, and she instantly guessed that he must be the valet of one of the new guests.

His quiet voice confirmed this.

"I am Mr. Beamish," he said. "I am the personal valet to Mr. Barnsby-Loxton. I arrived in a separate car, a few minutes after the gentlemen, but will take over from you now, if you please."

He stepped into the room, clearly wanting both of them out, pronto, so that he could resume his duties.

"Nice to meet you, Mr. Beamish," Mary said, as she and Hannah hustled out. They didn't get a reply, and Hannah waited until they were all the way down the stairs before she resumed her complaining.

"His valet seems just as nice as him," she remarked, in deeply sarcastic tones, causing Mary to snort.

"They're a right pair, aren't they?" she agreed. Then she sighed. "Oh, Hannah, this is looking so bad. What can we do?"

"I don't know!" Hannah sounded as agonized as Mary felt. "He was speaking badly about the place – but he was doing it to his equally snobbish friend, and not to the Drakeleys. He's probably a different person around them, and they're never going to see that side of him!"

"There must be a way of exposing who he really is," Mary said. "I'm sure if they'd heard him wishing for the place to be shelled, they'd feel differently."

"He said that?" As they hurried to the kitchens, Hannah sounded horrified.

"He did," Mary confirmed, and Hannah sighed.

"Well, you know, they might just laugh and say how brilliantly witty he is and thank him for pointing out that the roof needs some repairs. You know, people can be very tolerant when they think somebody's ready to save them."

"I'm going to keep tabs on him all the same," Mary resolved.

In fact, she had a new idea – one so audacious she didn't even dare share it with Hannah.

It involved the unlikeable Mr. Beamish – the man who must know all of Hugh Barnsby-Loxton's secrets. After dinner, when the men were having their brandies and cigars, she was going to see if she could get more information, and even some compromising evidence, from the snobbish and unlikeable valet. If she could ask the right questions without arousing his suspicions, she might just find what she was looking for.

CHAPTER NINE

It was after dinner, and the castle was already quieting down for the night, when Mary sneaked out of bed, wearing her slippers, so that the sound of her footfalls wouldn't attract any attention. She needed to stay quiet and sneaky and out of sight until she'd found where Beamish the valet was.

He was obviously staying on site, and would probably be in one of the spare rooms for servants, that were on the basement floor in the castle's other wing.

But Mary hoped, right now, he'd be in the staff tearoom. After all, he must have had a long day, unpacking, and attending to Hugh's wardrobe, and most likely, waiting for him to come back to his room to pack away his things when dinner was over. She knew how these bossy, obnoxious people treated their servants. It was likely that Beamish had to be at Hugh's beck and call until the moment his employer's spiky brown-haired head hit the pillow.

She thought her plans were going to succeed as she approached the tea room and heard the clink of a fork on a plate. But when she stuck her head around the door, she saw it was one of the other kitchen maids who'd worked late cleaning the kitchen after everything was packed away. That was a job they all took turns with – tomorrow, it was Mary's turn.

"Hello," she greeted her. "Have you seen anyone else around here since you got here?"

"Nope, it's just me," the maid replied, looking up from her slice of fruit cake. "Why?"

"Just wondered," Mary said cagily, and turned away.

Heading back along the corridor, she heard voices coming from the smoking room, and paused, listening. Maybe Hannah had been wrong, and Hugh would end up incriminating himself after all by saying something unacceptable in public.

But as she listened outside the door, she realized she couldn't hear him at all. She picked up Gilbert's voice, and Duke Drakeley's, and she even recognized the timbre of Cameron's voice – he was in there, too. She heard one or two others speaking, their voices unfamiliar. But the one voice she didn't hear was the resounding, loud, arrogant voice of Hugh himself.

In fact, at one stage, she heard the Duke say, "Where's Hugh? Wasn't he supposed to be joining us?"

"Perhaps he's gone to bed already. Long day, you know, old boy," Cameron replied smoothly.

Hugh definitely wasn't in the smoking room, so he must be asleep already, and if his valet wasn't in the kitchen and was nowhere else to be found, he must also have retired to bed. Now would not be a good time to strike up a conversation with Beamish and try to get the lowdown on his employer. It would have to wait until tomorrow.

She turned away and headed back to her own bedroom, ready to get some shuteye, and reminding herself that tomorrow was a new day.

And it was going to be a better day for Diana. Mary promised herself that.

***

She was about to fall asleep when there was a soft tapping on her door. The sound got her sitting instantly upright, staring anxiously at the door.

Immersed in slumber, Hannah mumbled drowsily in the bed beside Mary, before turning over and going back to sleep again.

Mary got up and went to the door. Opening it a crack, she stared out at Diana.

Her first thought was, distraught as her friend appeared, she looked really beautiful tonight. Her dark hair had been wound around her head in a braid, and her make-up was perfect, with bright, bold lipstick that matched the color of the gown she wore, and gold earrings dangling from her ears.

Quickly, Mary slipped out and shut the door.

"What's up, Diana?" she asked. "How did the evening go? Is everything alright?"

She'd really made an effort for Hugh. Diana didn't usually dress up so beautifully.

"Mary, I need your advice," Diana whispered, her gaze looking haunted.

"Advice on what?" Mary said warily. Right now, there was a multitude of subjects that she didn't feel qualified, or ready, to offer advice on. And she was sure that Diana had at least one of those subjects in mind.

"The man I love – he was here tonight. At dinner," she said, and Mary drew in her breath, gasping.

"Here, at the party? Diana, how do you feel about that?"

She wondered who he was. Which of the other guests, whom she'd seen briefly if at all, had stolen Diana's heart? Now, thinking back, there were a couple of possible men that fit the bill, who had looked personable, friendly, and around the age of thirty. Feeling curious to know more, she wished she'd taken a closer look at them.

But then, a terrible thought occurred to her.

What if Gilbert was the beloved that Diana had spoken about?

He was the right age, and he was handsome, and he'd been at dinner, and he knew the family well. Worry filled her as she thought that this was not just likely, but logical.

"This man you're in love with, who was at dinner, I'd like to ask one question about him," she said casually, trying to control her nerves and ask the question in a quiet voice, but as if it didn't matter.

"What is that?" Diana asked with a frown, clearly wanting to keep her secret to herself.

"He's – he's not from up north, is he?"

"Why do you ask that?" Diana said, surprised.

"Just wondering," Mary replied, nerves seething inside her.

"He's not from up north," Diana replied, and Mary felt a wave of relief wash over her, so powerful it left her weak. Whoever this man was, he wasn't Gilbert.

"I see," she said, trying to think of a reason to explain why she'd asked. "I won't ask for any further clues. I was just curious to know why he was here at this time."

Her friend sighed. "I invited him. I couldn't help myself. I told my mother he was another old school friend who was from the area, and so we should ask him to be here. I – I love him so! I don't know if I can go through with this engagement. To do it with him there, watching? To break both of our hearts? We spoke for a while in the library after dinner, and we – we have such a connection. He's the man I want to be with. Even for my family, can I ruin my own life this way? He suggested – well, we had this wild idea that we could elope tonight. Just run away, get married, and then face the music together. What do you think of that idea?"

Mary considered it for a few moments. "I can see why it's appealing to you," she said. But the words caused her a flicker of hope. Was Diana seriously rethinking? Did she have the courage to tell her parents she wasn't going to obey their wishes?

Diana fidgeted with the skirt of her dress, her fingers creasing and twisting the shiny silken fabric.

"There are pros and cons. But that's how desperate I'm starting to feel now."

"You really need to do what makes you happy," Mary urged her. "Follow your heart."

From somewhere far away down the corridor, she heard a door close, and they both looked around.

"You'd better get some rest, and I should go. Tomorrow's going to be very busy," Diana said. "I guess – I guess I just wanted to tell somebody my wild, mad idea."

"How did Hugh behave to you tonight?" Mary asked, wanting to find out before Diana left.

She still hoped he might show his true colors to the family, and they would decide the marriage was a bad decision.

"He was the same he always is," she said. "He's a loudmouth and a braggart and he talks nonstop about this mission he completed during the war, in Normandy. Listening to him, you'd swear he singlehandedly won the war. It gets more exaggerated and unlikely every time." Contempt dripped from her voice. "It was a relief when he went off to have brandies and cigars with the other men. At least it stopped me from perishing with boredom at hearing that story for a fourth time!"

She rolled her eyes before squeezing Mary's hand and turning away.

Mary frowned as she watched Diana retreat down the corridor.

There was an inconsistency she was picking up here. Diana clearly thought Hugh had been in the smoking room, but she knew he hadn't been there.

Where had he been? Was he up to something?

Tomorrow, Mary decided, was going to be the day she blew Hugh Barnsby-Loxton's secrets all the way into the open. If it broke up the engagement or inspired Diana to change her mind and elope with her true love, then so much the better.

CHAPTER TEN

"Are those petit-fours ready yet?"

The cook's frantic question resounded around the bustling kitchen, and Mary quickly took a moment to look, stepping away from her task of carving five large roast chickens, and peeking into the oven to see if the cakes were ready to come out.

"Another five minutes, I think," she called back, and then focused anew on her efforts.

There had been so much to do today! Ever since her feet had touched the ground just before five a.m., the day had been a nonstop whirl of activity. As well as the formal dinner, the Drakeleys had scheduled a lunch including other friends and neighbors, seeing that the weather was fine and it would be pleasant for them to travel a few miles there and back.

It meant a mammoth task of food preparation, with breakfast, lunch and dinner, with breakfast and dinner for twenty, and lunch for double that number.

Finally, the last of the chickens were arranged on the platter, and the luncheon plating could begin.

Now, working with the other maids, while the cook tended to the petit-fours for the dinner menu, the chicken had to be placed on the guests' plates, each with a serving of creamy risotto, mashed spicy pumpkin, a light gravy, and a crispy crouton.

Plating up for lunch was Mary's job, and she focused on it intently, making sure every plate looked neat, attractive, and uniform.

Chicken, risotto, pumpkin, crouton – and the gravy in the right place.

She was getting into the rhythm of it, repeating the action again and again just as if she was back in a factory – but this time a food factory.

And then, suddenly, her concentration was broken.

"Excuse me," a sharp voice said, from just behind her shoulder.

Mary glanced up from her frantic preparation.

Beamish, the valet, was standing there and staring critically down at the plates of food.

"Mr. Beamish?" Mary said, trying her best to summon up some charm and politeness. After all, she had been looking for the valet yesterday, and now, here he was. Perhaps he'd inadvertently let something slip about Hugh that she could use to influence the course of events.

It might even be fortuitous that he was here now, because she'd been so busy that she hadn't had a chance to set foot out of the kitchen, or do any research, at all.

"I wanted to make sure that the food is up to Mr. Barnsby-Loxton's standards," he said haughtily, causing Mary to bristle instantly. "Last night's menu was disappointing to him and he could barely eat it."

"It's all been prepared to the highest standards," she said in cool tones, but even she could hear the edge of annoyance in her voice that she simply couldn't suppress.

"I'm sure it has," he said sarcastically. "But Mr. Barnsby-Loxton is on a strict diet. His digestion is sensitive after the heroic escapade in Normandy where he was forced to survive on canned frog's legs and cheap red wine, for a prolonged period, while in hiding. The experience scarred him, and now, there are certain foodstuffs he will not eat."

"Like what?" Mary asked, remembering what Diana had said about the story getting exaggerated over time. Frog's legs and wine? Seriously?

Beamish began counting on his fingers. "Chicken, for a start. Risotto. Pumpkin."

That left the crouton and the gravy, Mary realized, now beginning to panic.

And worse still, she was right in the middle of service! There were now three serving maids standing and waiting for her to plate up so that the next round of guests could be served.

She wanted to say, "But why?"

Why, after surviving on frog's legs, did this dislikeable man claim he couldn't eat chicken or rice? It didn't make sense. Was Beamish just here to cause trouble and draw more attention to Hugh's war exploits? Mary was beginning to suspect that he had literally looked at the plate and named all the ingredients on it. Maybe the only reason he hadn't added the crouton to the list was that he felt unsure about how to pronounce it.

But to argue her theory would waste precious time. And it would be an argument she would lose.

40

"Can you give me a moment?" she said. "I have to get these plates done. As soon as they're done, I'll see what I can offer Mr. Barnsby-Loxton as an alternative."

Beamish didn't even move away, but stayed right where he was, staring at her, as she feverishly worked to arrange the last few plates.

Then, instead of finally taking a small but well-earned rest before starting to focus on dinner, she had to rush off to the larder, followed by Beamish.

"Does your employer eat ham?" she asked.

"Ham, yes," he said.

"And – and bean salad?"

"I'm not sure about those particular beans. I think so."

She dished a spoon of bean salad onto the plate and added two thick, generous slices of ham. The meal looked spartan and plain compared to the variety on the other plates, but right now, she didn't have time to add anything more.

"There you go," she said. "There's bread in a basket near the kitchen door if you want to add a few slices, and some pats of butter there, too."

"I'll be back, closer to dinnertime," he threatened.

"Does Mr. Barnsby-Loxton eat roast beef, Yorkshire pudding, and roast potatoes?" she called out.

"I don't know," Beamish called back. "He will need to decide that, closer to the time."

"Where was he after dinner last night?"

Mary didn't have the courage to shout that question out. She muttered it to herself as she returned to her post at the kitchen counter, feeling frazzled. Today was really not going as planned. Apart from now adding 'insufferably fussy' to the list of Hugh's insufferable qualities, she still didn't have anything on him that would make the Drakeley family, as one, turn around and say, "This engagement is off!"

How was she going to sneak away and do some research? There didn't seem to be any time, and the clock was ticking inexorably forward to the engagement dinner. She guessed that after tapping on her door last night, Diana had rethought her plans to elope, because everything today was going ahead as planned, and she'd briefly seen Diana, passing the kitchens, with her head bowed.

"Mary!" The cook's voice cut into her thoughts. "Some rosemary from the herb garden, will you, please?"

"On my way!" she called back, changing her route and hurrying out of the kitchen.

The herb garden was in one of her favorite parts of the castle. Behind the main building, shielded by its stony walls from the northerly wind, with a view to the south over a patchwork of fields, some farmed, some fallow, framed in the distance by rolling, rugged hills. She was sure, in a few more weeks, that the fallow meadows would be filled with daisies and daffodils. The herbs were in a three-sided courtyard with beds on each of the three sides. In the middle was an ornamental stone seat.

As she rushed into the herb garden, heading straight for the rosemary bush, Mary noticed that one of the guests who had arrived yesterday, Diana's school friend that she didn't much like, was sitting on the bench.

"Good afternoon," she called cheerfully, picking a few large sprigs of rosemary and putting them into her basket.

There was no reply from the woman, and Mary assumed she hadn't heard, or wasn't going to acknowledge, the greeting. Some people didn't want servants to be visible and acknowledged in their lives, and that was just the way things were.

But, as she turned, she heard a muffled, heartfelt sob from the woman on the bench.

CHAPTER ELEVEN

That poignant sound caught all of Mary's attention, and she stared at the woman more closely.

She was crying, hard! Her face was buried in her cupped hands, and her shoulders were shuddering.

"Ma'am!" Mary's heart melted at the miserable sight. She should at least offer some help, or a handkerchief, or a cup of tea. "Are you all right?"

The woman glanced up. She was pretty – Mary had briefly taken in that fact yesterday when the car had arrived – and now, this afternoon, despite her tear streaked face, Mary saw she was really beautiful, with high cheekbones, a heart shaped face, and a wavy tumble of silvery blond hair. Emily was her name – she remembered now. Lady Emily somebody.

"I'm all right," Lady Emily said, in a hoarse, breaking voice.

"Is there anything I can get you?" she offered. "A glass of water, some tea – would a scone help?"

It was Mary's opinion that a good scone did help in most situations.

But she shook her head, letting out a low, mirthless laugh, which Mary assumed was prompted by the very idea that anything at all could help her.

"You could get me back the man I love?" she asked, somewhat cynically. And then, as if unable to stop the words and needing to share her misery, she continued in a rush. "Because yesterday, he told me once and for all, that we will not marry, and we'll never be together."

"Oh, no! Oh, dear. I'm so very sorry!" Mary clasped the basket's handle tightly, wishing she could do more to help. What a terrible predicament. This poor woman had – well, it sounded as if she'd actually been turned down by the man she loved. And here she was, at an engagement celebration? That was a very difficult situation to be in, given the circumstances.

Although Lady Emily would be wrong if she thought there was love and romance in the air and that Diana was getting betrothed to the love of her life – she probably was thinking that was the case, and feeling extra miserable because of it.

"It's life, I suppose. I should have known I'd never have him," she said, now with a touch of anger in her voice that made Mary think she was starting to overcome the worst of her misery. Anger wasn't a nice emotion, but it did help to take the worst of the sting out of heartbreak, she acknowledged.

It wasn't really her place to discuss this further, and she had the feeling that if she did ask more questions, Lady Emily would shut down, or else, she would later regret having confided too much in a mere maid.

"I'm sorry again, and please, come by the kitchens if there's anything you need," she said, by way of politely wrapping up this conversation.

Blinking tears away, Lady Emily stared sullenly into the distance without replying, and Mary quickly headed inside.

There, to her surprise, she found Cameron Pratt. He was standing at the kitchen door and staring inside in a hopeful way.

Rushing over to help him, Mary asked, "Is there anything I can help you with, sir?"

"Why, yes, thank you," he said, in a refined voice. When he wasn't with his boorish friend, he seemed a little nicer – at any rate, he was able to be polite and courteous. "I'm hoping I might be able to get some coffee. I'm in need of a pick-me-up, since I didn't sleep well and there's a long day ahead."

"Of course. Can I bring a jug up to your room?"

"I can take it myself if you prepare it," he said, moving into the kitchen. Mary noticed, now that she was paying attention to him, that he walked with a slight limp.

"Did you hurt yourself?" she asked, wondering if he'd twisted his ankle, or stubbed his toe, in which case a hot water bottle, or a bag of ice, might also be in order.

But he shook his head and said, briefly, "Old war injury. It flares up when I travel."

"I'm sorry," Mary said, and rushed off to organize the jug of coffee.

She brought it back and handed the tray to him, and he carried it out with another polite thank you. And then, it was time for her to return to her station, because there was more frenzied preparation under way for the dinner.

There were three large salmon that had to be scaled, cleaned, deboned, and then flaked up ready for the long, slow cooking and mixing in the soup. Fish prep was Mary's least favorite job, and it was one which required an eagle eyed attention to detail.

One bone – just one bone left in the soup, could ruin a guest's meal and also result in a nasty choking incident. She worked with knife and tweezers, being careful not to waste any of the expensive fish. But as she worked, she felt more and more frustrated. If only she'd been able to tell Hannah more about what she'd planned. If only she'd had the chance to tell Gilbert!

He'd helped her before in an investigation, although it had been reluctantly offered at first. But there was surely the chance he'd be ready to help her again. The right word at the right time, spoken in company, might prod the unlikeable Hugh into revealing his true character.

Although her stomach churned as she considered that possibility. She didn't know where Gilbert's loyalties lay, and the Drakeleys were family friends. He might agree with the Duke and Duchess that the wedding was a good thing, and think it was Diana who was being unreasonable.

She didn't know him well enough to ask, and so she couldn't ask, she concluded reluctantly. It was just as well she wouldn't have the chance, because what if things went horribly wrong?

Finally, the last of the fish was done, and the shreds of salmon were simmering in the fragrant broth, rich with the infusion of celery and onion, and the addition of vast amounts of cream.

"You're on that broth, right?" the cook asked. "Get in there with the masher, and make sure that salmon's as fine as can be. We can pass it through a couple of sieves when it's cooled down. We need this to be a good, creamy, quality soup.

It looked like she was in sole charge of the soup – and to her consternation, Mary saw that the time was already nearly six p.m. Luncheon had been over hours ago. That fish prep had taken an excessive amount of time. Her legs were aching just as hard as they'd done when she'd been at the factory, and her arms were stiff from the nonstop effort of scaling, deboning, shredding and mashing – and now in one short hour, the guests would be congregating for canapés.

Now, the physical punishment of having to work extra hard, due to the Drakeleys being so short staffed, was taking its toll.

Guests, dressed in their evening finery, were already flitting in and out of the kitchen, and there was the valet back again. Yes, now familiar with the location of her workstation, he was heading over to her.

45

"What soup is that?" Beamish demanded loudly.

Several of the kitchen staff looked around in surprise at his sharp tone.

"It's cream of salmon soup," Mary replied, waiting for the inevitable. She was not disappointed.

"Unfortunately," Beamish said, "Mr. Barnsby-Loxton does not eat salmon soup."

What a surprise, Mary thought.

"We also have vegetable soup, and cream of celery soup, in the cold room," she said, having prepared for what she'd say, while she'd been shredding the fish. "Which of those would Mr. Barnsby-Loxton prefer? They are the only options." She made sure to speak with a note of calm authority.

The valet looked miffed, as if Mary had taken all the fun out of an encounter he'd been looking forward to.

"My employer is circulating with the dinner guests. I'll go and ask," he said abruptly, and turned away. In what seemed like no time at all, punctuated from Mary's side by feverish mashing of the soup, he was back.

"Cream of celery soup will do," he said.

"I'll make him a separate pot," Mary replied.

She hurried to the cold room and got out the container of cold cream of celery soup. She ladled a big helping into a bowl, took it through to the kitchen, and put it in its own tiny pot on the back of the stove, to warm slowly.

Then she was called over to the other side of the kitchen to help with the canapés. The levels of activity were frenetic. Two footmen were waiting to take through the trays. Mary arranged deviled eggs, chipolata sausages, and cheese pastry tartlets in as artistic a way as she could, before the trays were whisked through.

Then, from the back of the kitchen, disaster. The shriek of a maid signaled that a tray had been dropped!

Rushing over to help, Mary saw in consternation that it was one of the trays of roast potatoes. Now, oily potatoes littered the floor – and there was a risk they were going to be short at dinner. A frenzy of cleaning up followed, and Mary began peeling and parboiling another batch of potatoes as if her life depended on it.

"Cut 'em smaller than usual, so they'll roast up quicker," the cook advised, already preparing a tray with a thick coating of goose fat.

And then, it was back to her side of the kitchen again to check the soups.

"First course! We need first course out, now!" the butler called.

Frantically, Mary pulled off her apron, which was spattered and smeared, and pulled on the fresh one that the cook handed her. She began ladling out the soups, one bowl at a time, making sure each one looked the same, finishing the bowls with a scattering of parsley and a pinch of paprika.

Bowl after bowl – and then they were done. Seeing just two were remaining, including Hugh's special soup, she took them both, and headed through to the dining room herself. She wondered if she might be lucky enough to serve Gilbert, since she hadn't set eyes on him all day.

The dining room was splendidly arrayed. Hannah and her team must have been working like demons today, Mary acknowledged. The deep red curtains looked all the more glamorous thanks to the sets of candelabras, with brightly burning candles placed along the sideboard. The long wooden table, covered with a brilliant white cloth, was set with sparkling silverware, with arrangements of red roses set along the length of the table.

If only the occasion had been as wonderful as the décor clearly was, she thought, listening to the sounds of a piano coming from the drawing room next door, where somebody had been hired to play throughout dinner.

Sure enough, Hugh and Gilbert were the only two guests still waiting for soup.

Mary hurried over, and carefully placed the first bowl in front of Gilbert. She breathed in the faint scent of sandalwood that she remembered from the last time she'd been close to him. He glanced up, and she saw his grin.

"Why, thank you," he muttered. "I've missed you today. I looked in on the kitchens, but you were working so hard you didn't even notice me."

"Missed you too," she breathed, her heart automatically speeding up as she revealed just a little of the feelings in it. Then, she moved two places to the side, and served Hugh his cream of celery soup.

"It was an extremely dangerous military maneuver," he bragged, stirring the soup with his spoon, "but I can say without a doubt it won us the war. It involved me spending a week in a concrete bunker, having bypassed enemy lines, waiting for the right moment to strike!

Hidden away in that bunker, I could have been slaughtered at any moment by the French. I lived on half a tin of escargots and a bottle of white vinegar."

He shoveled a large mouthful of soup into his mouth before reaching for the salt.

What had happened to the frog's legs and the cheap red wine he'd mentioned last time? If Mary had allowed her eyes to boggle, they would have boggled. He was embellishing this ridiculous story well past the point of reality. She was not one to downplay the bravery involved in such a maneuver – but exaggerating a story each time, and changing it this way, didn't make the teller seem any braver. In her opinion, anyway.

She saw Diana, looking miserable and resigned, stifle a yawn. Across the table, even Cameron, Hugh's friend and fellow soldier, was fidgeting, downing a gulp of his wine and then bending down to rub his leg, as if his war injury was paining him.

Hurrying back to the kitchen, she left the boring war story behind, checking on the roast potatoes and giving the gravy a stir.

And then, already, it was time to rush back into the dining room and collect the soup bowls.

"A toast!" Duke Drakeley rose to his feet with a scrape of his chair as the maids entered, interrupting Hugh mid-sentence – he must have been telling the war story yet again – and causing him to glower. "A toast to the official betrothal of my beloved daughter Diana, to the wonderful and courageous man, somebody who is dear to our family and whom we have known for almost all of his twenty-five years – Hugh Barnsby-Loxton. As of this moment, I welcome you to our family. The engagement is announced!"

The butlers rushed in with champagne, filling glasses as people downed the contents in one gulp. Cheers rang out. Applause resounded around the dining room. Smiling, the guests all looked at Hugh and Diana.

As she collected up the bowls, Mary saw that Diana was sitting as if turned to stone, a smile pasted on her face that from a mile away, with a pang of sympathy, Mary could see was little more than a grimace.

As for Hugh, he raised his glass and made his own toast, which Mary picked up over the sound of cheers.

"To my title," he said, and then, louder, "To our engagement!"

Hugh downed his champagne and then stuck his spoon into the soup bowl for a last mouthful as the maid waited to take his plate. He shoveled it into his mouth without looking as if he was even tasting it or caring about it. And he hadn't glanced at Diana once, nor shown her any affection whatsoever.

Mary felt her heart shattering as she turned away, preparing to leave.

And then, a sudden, loud, guttural choke from the dining table made her turn back again in alarm.

Hugh Barnsby-Loxton was no longer finishing up his soup. Instead, he was clutching his throat with a look of deep alarm in his eyes.

His face had turned even more brick red than it was a minute ago, and cries of consternation resounded from around the table as he choked again.

CHAPTER TWELVE

"He's choking!" Shouts of concern, stating the obvious, rang in the air, and Mary froze, staring at the scene, feeling a sense of deep foreboding at what was playing out. This looked serious!

Gilbert jumped up and ran to him, slapping him on the back, but the choking did not ease. Now, Hugh was clutching at his throat.

"It's a fishbone. They must have left a bone in the soup!" one of the women cried.

"He had a special soup!" Mary shouted, adding her voice to the commotion. "Cream of celery. There isn't a bone in any of the soups, though!"

She knew what she said was defensive and unnecessary, but she had to say something. This man was choking and whatever it was, was refusing to budge.

"I'll get a glass of water!"

She didn't think water would help – she was seriously doubtful that a mere sip of water would ease such a serious bout of coughing. It was as if Hugh couldn't get any air at all. But at least it gave her something to do instead of watching this terrible scene, feeling utterly helpless and somehow responsible.

She rushed back to the kitchen, heart hammering, a little voice inside her telling her that if she got the water really, really fast it might avert the disaster that she feared was coming.

Taking a glass from the array of clean ones on the drying rack, Mary poured water from the tap in the kitchen, her hands shaking with haste and tension, a splash of the icy cold water spilling over her hand.

And then she was rushing back, hearing that the cries had died down now, and that only a terrible silence, and a few sobs, came from the brightly lit hall. Even the pianist had stopped playing.

Mary burst into the room, holding the glass in front of her. And there, she stopped, staring in horror at the sight.

Hugh was on the floor, with Gilbert and Duke Drakeley bent over him. Brick red a minute ago, his face was now waxy pale. His eyes were wide and staring. And, as she watched, Gilbert checked his pulse, placing two fingers over the portion of Hugh's wrist that was visible from the sleeve of his smart black dinner jacket.

"He's dead," Gilbert said.

His face was frozen in horror as he glanced up at Mary. That look wasn't one she'd ever wanted to see in the eyes of a man that she had developed a fondness for. Gilbert's expression looked like – well, it looked for a moment like he was staring at a stranger.

"Look at the color of his skin, and the foam around his lips," Duke Drakeley snapped, in a steely, accusatory voice. "This is no ordinary death. This man has been poisoned!"

Flat and final, the words resounded around the dining room, seeming just as loud as the cheers had done earlier.

Mary dropped the glass. She didn't even realize she'd done so until it smashed on the floor – it had slipped from her fingers without her even noticing as she stared at the shocking scene, feeling sick inside.

One of the women – she thought it was Hugh's mother – let out a small scream and reeled backward in her chair, her husband leaping to his feet to grab her. There were gasps and sobs and scrapes of chairs. And then, Mary felt her arm taken in a tight, inexorable grasp.

It was Duchess Drakeley, and she looked utterly furious. There was an expression in her eyes that Mary had never seen there before.

"Come with me," she said. "We're locking you away while we wait for the police!"

"But – but –"

There was no time or room for argument. Mary turned her back on the shocked diners, whose attention was now divided between the dead man on the deep blue carpet, and herself.

She had time only for a desperate, devastated glance at Gilbert, seeing the same horror in his own eyes as she felt in her heart.

And then, she was being led out of the dining room, her arm relentlessly held, as if she was a criminal – or a killer.

"I – I didn't do it," she said breathlessly as Duchess Drakeley marched her along, shouting out for the housekeeper as she passed the kitchens. The staff had realized there was a crisis, probably caused by Mary's frantic foray into the kitchen a minute ago. They were crowding to the door, looking wide-eyed and concerned. Miss Hobbs, who'd also been helping with the dinner service, pushed her way through the melee and joined them, walking on Mary's other side, as Duchess Drakeley updated her in a taut, stressed voice.

"This kitchen maid served Diana's fiancé a bowl of poisoned soup. We are locking her away until the police come."

"In the small study, ma'am?" The housekeeper's voice was guarded. Even in her confusion and trauma, Mary wondered if she thought Mary was as guilty as Duchess Drakeley did.

"Yes. That will suit perfectly."

The room was up two flights of stairs at the end of the passage on the right. Duchess Drakeley marched her inside, while the housekeeper moved the key from the inside of the door, to the outside.

"Please, wait!" Mary begged, but the door slammed, and a moment later, the lock rattled as the key turned.

Wild-eyed, she took a look around the room that was now her prison. It contained a wooden desk, an armchair, a leather-upholstered antique chair, and a bookcase with old, scholarly-looking tomes. There was a window, but Mary couldn't possibly escape through it. Examining her options, scarce as they were, she reminded herself that this room was on the third floor. It was pitch dark, and escaping through a window right now would only confirm to everybody that she was guilty of this crime.

There was nothing for her to do but sit tight and wait.

She slumped down on the antique chair, resting her arms on the desk, letting out a deep sigh and shivering with horror as she did so.

She simply could not believe how this evening had gone so bad, so fast. One minute she'd been serving soup and feeling terrible for poor, sad Diana. The next minute, there was a dead body on the floor and thanks to her tireless preparation in the kitchen, and the fact she'd handed Hugh his bowl, she was now the prime suspect for the murder.

Dragged out of the dining hall in front of all the guests – including Gilbert!

Mary had never felt more anguished in all her life.

It felt like only a few seconds had passed, but it must have been longer, when she heard voices approach outside, and brisk footsteps.

"This is the room where she is for now," the housekeeper's voice rang out. "We've locked it, of course. Here's the key. I'll bring you some tea shortly, officer."

The lock rattled, and the door swung open.

Mary stared in consternation at the uniformed man who was framed in the doorway.

He stared at her in equal surprise.

"You!" they said simultaneously, blinking in shock.

CHAPTER THIRTEEN

Never had Mary thought that she'd recognize this policeman, but she did. It was Constable Philpott, the tall, blond, officious-looking officer who'd handled the very first case she had been caught up in. Then, as now, she'd unfortunately ended up being a suspect.

Constable Philpott had embraced the idea of her guilt with what Mary thought to be an excessive amount of enthusiasm. While giving respectful consideration to everyone who thought she'd been the murderer, his lack of motivation to find any alternative suspects had been most disappointing.

In fact, she'd decided that it was a character flaw.

She'd finally been cleared, and one of the reasons she had felt very grateful to be moving to this isolated castle, which was set high in the Midlands hills, was that it was far, far away from where Constable Philpott worked.

And now, here he was?

"What are you doing here?" she blurted out.

It might be rude for a suspect to ask the first question, but Mary simply couldn't help those heartfelt words.

"I might ask you the same," he said, turning and closing the door before walking over to the armchair. He looked down at it, and then over at the desk.

Clearly, he thought that being in the armchair while she was seated at the desk, was a compromising position that put him at a disadvantage. It was as if she could read the thoughts that were slowly forming behind his pale blue, fishy eyes.

He had the same neat, but slanted, fringe of hair under his helmet that she remembered from before, as if he'd used scissors at home, while peering into his bathroom mirror.

Well, she wasn't moving out of her seat for him. She tightened her lips, ready to fight out this small but significant battle of wills. He was here to ask her questions! It wasn't like she was a naughty child, and he the headmaster.

Reluctantly, Constable Philpott sat down in the armchair and took out his notebook.

"I'm here because I found work at the castle," Mary said, already hearing the note of defensiveness in her voice.

"And I'm here because I now work at the local police station in Little Brayshire," Philpott said. "There was a position open here, and they were looking for a constable. It came with a promotion and a small but significant salary increase, so I applied. And thanks to my successful role in the investigation at Coldstream Lodge, where you were, I got the job."

"But –" Mary clamped her lips together, because if she said anything, this was going to turn into an argument. Philpott had suspected the wrong person the whole way through, and she had ended up solving the crime herself.

But it wouldn't do to make an enemy of the constable, she told herself. Even though her emotions were running high and she wanted to shout and scream and tell him he'd been pretty useless throughout that entire investigation, not to mention wet behind the ears and totally inexperienced, now was the time for prudence.

As her mum had always said, being polite never made a situation worse.

"Well, I'm glad to hear you were promoted, and congratulations," she said.

"And congratulations on your job, here at Castle Drakeley," he said, to her surprise.

Then his gaze returned to his notebook.

"It seems, however, that your job hasn't gone exactly as planned?" he said. "I have several accounts, both from the duchess, and from members of staff, who have said that you were making, and serving, the soup which the deceased, Mr. Barnsby-Loxton, partook of just before his death. It's definitely poisoned, by the way," he said. "We've sent the rest of the contents of the pot off for testing, but there's no doubt, from his inflamed throat and the rapid onset of his demise, that it was caused by that soup. My personal feeling is that it was hemlock. We've had a few cases of accidental poisoning over the years, in this precinct, because it grows in the area. But I've sent the dregs of the soup off to be tested."

Mary breathed deeply, reminding herself to stay calm and logical.

"I was responsible for heating up the soup, after Mr. Barnsby-Loxton's valet, Beamish, came to the kitchens to tell me that he didn't eat salmon soup, which the rest of the guests were being served."

"Is that so?" There was interest in his pale blue eyes as he regarded her.

"I immediately went to the cold room to see what we could substitute. After discussion with the valet," – it wouldn't hurt at all to mention him a few times, Mary thought, and could only widen the net of suspicion, "we decided on the cream of celery soup. I put a serving in a small pot, and then I placed it at the back of the stove to warm."

"And then you served it?"

He was skipping a step, something which, in the circumstances, Mary could not allow him to do.

"Are you a cook at all, Constable Philpott?" she asked.

He paused, looking surprised and somewhat taken aback. "I can – I can heat up a pot of soup or beans, as well as anybody else," he replied, and now there was a slightly defensive tone to his voice.

"You'll know, then, that if you put a pot on a low heat, it doesn't require much attention as it warms slowly," she said.

He was looking thoughtful now, nodding in a way that hinted to Mary some personal soul-searching was happening.

"I think that might be where I've been going wrong," he said. "A low heat, you say? And then the stuff doesn't burn as soon as you take your eye off it?"

"It was one of the first things they taught me here at the castle," Mary said. "Low and slow is the way to go when reheating anything."

Philpott drew himself up. "Interesting as this may be, how is it relevant to this murder? What are you trying to argue, by saying this, Miss Adams?"

"The soup was set on the coolest part of the stove and required none of my attention," she said. "And there were about a hundred other jobs to do. I left it alone." She remembered the catastrophe that had drawn them all to the back of the kitchen. A catastrophe that she now realized provided her with a small, but possibly significant, alibi.

"Just after I set the soup to warm, one of the maids dropped a tray of roast potatoes at the back of the kitchen," she told him. "We all rushed there to clean up the mess, and then I was in charge of peeling and slicing a whole new bag. That meant I was standing at the back counter, with my back to the room. It was chaos, everyone was rushing around trying to get the last minute prep done. Anyone could have come in and dropped that poison into the soup."

He thought about that, tapping his pen on the notepad.

"But how would anyone else have known that soup was his?" he asked.

There again, Mary was deeply relieved to have an answer.

"Because his valet went and asked him what his preference was, in front of all the other guests, during pre-dinner drinks," she said. "Every single person who was in that room would have known that Hugh Barnsby-Loxton was the only person having cream of celery soup tonight." She took a deep breath. "I didn't even know the victim, and I barely spoke to him. He only arrived yesterday. He's from a community that all know each other and somebody else, not me, must have had a reason for killing him."

Speaking firmly, she looked the constable straight in the eye.

She'd done her absolute best to clear herself. In Mary's opinion, her own version provided a strong reason why he shouldn't suspect her.

Unless he'd heard from somebody that Mary knew Diana hadn't wanted to marry the unlikeable man.

If he had heard that, Mary realized with a twist of her stomach, then she was sunk.

For a long, tense moment, the only sound was the scribbling of Constable Philpott's pen, and the rustle of the page.

Then, Philpott looked up, giving a firm nod.

He'd made his decision, and she waited for the words that would either seal her fate – or give her a temporary stay of execution.

CHAPTER FOURTEEN

"What you have told me has some merit," Philpott said, rather reluctantly, as Mary's fingernails dug into her palms. "I'm going to go and speak to the family again. There are some points within your version that need confirming."

Mary's mouth went instantly dry. They wouldn't refuse to confirm the truth, in their rage and grief, would they? Especially with Hugh's parents actually sitting there. They might decide that getting somebody behind bars for this murder as soon as possible, was the best course of action – and who better to lock away, than the maid who'd prepared the food?

Constable Philpott struggled up, with some difficulty, from the soft, low-slung armchair, and then walked out of the room. As he opened the door, Mary heard another voice from outside. It was the housekeeper again.

"Ah, Constable! I've just brought your tea!" Miss Hobbs exclaimed.

That was too much of a coincidence for Mary to believe. Tea didn't take that long to prepare. Mary knew instinctively that the housekeeper had been listening at the door, keen to pick up as much as possible about what was happening inside the small study. Mary wondered how soundproof that door was, and how much she'd heard.

At any rate, Philpott said, "You can take the tray to the parlor. I'll be speaking to the family there."

The key turned in the lock. It was clear that he still didn't trust her. Her fate hung in the balance, and it all depended on what the family said.

Mary waited. There was only silence outside the room. The study was icy cold, and she shivered, wrapping her arms around herself. Eventually, she moved to the armchair, whose leather embrace felt slightly warmer than the cold, hard seat of the desk chair. Slipping off her shoes, she curled her stockinged feet under her for warmth, and snuggled up against the cushion, waiting and listening for any sound.

She hadn't thought she'd ever be able to nod off at such a time, but somehow, she managed to slip into a light doze. At any rate, by the time the door rattled again, she was jerked from a strange conversation where she'd been explaining to Constable Philpott exactly how to make cream of celery soup.

Sitting bolt upright, she stared warily at the door as it opened.

It was Diana. She was carrying a big, padded jacket, and a knee rug. And under her other arm, Mary saw a flask of tea.

"I'm so, so sorry about this!" Diana was still wearing her elegant sky blue evening gown, but she'd put a large woolen coat over it, and she had warm boots on her feet instead of the strappy sandals she'd worn earlier. "I cannot believe this has happened. It's a catastrophe. For you, I mean."

"Oh, thank you so much for the tea and the jacket!" Mary was literally shivering as she wrapped it around her, opened the flask, and took a gulp of the hot, sweet tea.

"It's like this whole situation turned into a huge, weird nightmare. I just do not understand this," she said.

Mary nodded. She was wholeheartedly grateful for her friend's loving care at such a time.

"I'm very worried that your family is going to insist I'm arrested," she said miserably. "They believe I must be the killer, because I heated and served the soup."

But Diana shook her head adamantly, as she sat down on the floor next to Mary's armchair, wrapping her hands around her knees.

"I've spent the last hour telling them that everyone was in the kitchen for some reason, during the evening, and all of us heard that Hugh was getting a separate serving of soup. I think they're finally coming around to the fact that you aren't the only person who could have done it. I mean, they don't think you're innocent," she added uneasily. "But they are at least ready to look at who else it might have been."

"Do you have any idea?" Mary asked.

Diana shook her head. "I've no idea. Hugh's parents are incredibly upset. The more so because it happened just after the announcement of the engagement."

Mary frowned, not understanding the significance. "I know it must be even more heartbreaking for them at such a poignant moment," she said, hoping that it was the right thing to say.

"It's not the poignancy that is upsetting them," Diana said, and her dismissive tone told Mary more about her feelings for her future parents in law, than words could have done.

She listened carefully as Diana continued.

"What's upsetting them is that the agreement clearly stated that the first hundred acres would go to my parents as soon as the engagement was announced. And that happened. Hugh only died afterward. So, my parents get the land, and the Barnsby-Loxtons are horribly angry about it. They seem to think you did it, but that you were asked to, or paid to, by one of us. We all ended up having a huge fight about it, but at least it casts some doubt on the situation."

"Oh, my goodness!" Mary said. Things were more complicated than they'd first seemed. Perhaps even an investigator as narrow minded as Constable Philpott might end up stumbling over these important details, and taking them into account. Especially if the families were bickering and accusing each other while seated in the parlor.

She so badly wanted to ask Diana how Gilbert had reacted after this death, but Diana probably wouldn't know, and she didn't want to talk about the relationship between herself and Gilbert at such a time.

But whoever this killer was, Mary felt frankly devastated that such a crime had to happen in front of Hugh's parents as well as everybody else. Even though she was desperate not to end up unfairly accused, she couldn't help a surge of sympathy toward everyone who had known and loved this man.

"I think they're going to come back just now and let you out, anyway," Diana said. "And Mary, I feel – well, I feel so bad about all of this."

She sighed, and looking at her gaunt face and reddened eyes, Mary saw for the first time what a toll these events had taken on her friend. She reached out and squeezed her hand. Mary's fingers, slightly warmed from the flask of tea, were warmer than Diana's, which felt icy.

"I hope we find out the truth soon."

"The truth?" Diana frowned. "Yes, I certainly hope we do." She looked at Mary. "And I need to tell you, now – I did what you advised. I decided to follow my heart."

Mary's eyes widened, but she didn't have the chance to ask Diana what she meant. The slamming of a door from down the corridor signaled that people were coming back, and after giving her hand one last squeeze, Diana quickly slipped out of the room, turning the other way, so that whoever was approaching wouldn't see her.

A few moments later, the door opened again, and Mary struggled to her feet. This armchair really was very awkward to get out of, and she needed to stand, because along with Constable Philpott, Duchess Drakeley was now entering the room.

"Miss Adams," Philpott said, sounding as brisk and officious as if he'd just woken in the morning from a good night's rest. In fact, it was nearly three a.m., according to the clock on the wall. "I've been speaking to everybody who's involved in tonight's proceedings. This is a complex case. It's going to require a skilled investigator to solve it."

He didn't go as far as tapping his chest while he spoke, but Mary felt the intent was there.

"Given the complexity, we've agreed that you can be released and return to your duties. However," his voice was stern, "you are forbidden to leave the castle. You must remain indoors, and must not attempt to run, hide, or hinder the investigation in any way."

Duchess Drakeley raised her chin. "Do we have your word on this, Miss Adams?" she asked, her quivering voice showing the strain she'd endured over the past few hours.

"You have my word," Mary said respectfully.

"Then you can go to your room and report for duty in the morning. Hopefully this – this whole sorry business is over by then."

With her voice breaking, Duchess Drakeley turned and swept from the room.

"Thank you," Mary said humbly to Constable Philpott, as she passed.

"You're not off the hook yet," he warned her. "And I need you to obey the instructions you've been given to remain on the premises. If I remember, there were times in the last case I handled involving you when you disobeyed those same orders."

"I promise I'll remain inside," Mary said.

But as she left, she felt a quiver of unease. The conversation she'd had with Diana was preying on her mind, and Mary could not help a dark suspicion forming.

The only person she knew of who had a strong motive for wanting Hugh Barnsby-Loxton dead, and who knew the terms of the contract that had allowed the Drakeleys to gain one hundred acres of additional farmland – was Diana Drakeley herself.

Just before she left, she'd told Mary that she had followed her heart.

Now, Mary was wondering uneasily what that had involved.

CHAPTER FIFTEEN

Never had Mary been so relieved to push open the door to her shared basement bedroom. She was quivering with exhaustion, and her eyes felt dry and reddened. Even a couple of hours of shuteye would be helpful, she hoped, and make her feel less like a quivering wreck.

Although she tried her best to open the door silently, it made its usual squeak.

And at that squeak, Hannah sat bolt upright, staring at the door.

"Mary!" she whispered. "You got out of there! I thought you'd be in prison. I was so, so worried!"

To Mary's surprise, Hannah jumped right out of bed and gave her an enormous hug, which just about squeezed the breath out of her.

"Well, I'm not cleared," she whispered back, speaking as softly as she possibly could, because it was clear that the household staff were all agog for information surrounding this crime and had no compunction about listening at doors. "But they do see it may have been somebody else, so for now, I'm still able to continue working."

"We all went to bed after it happened," Hannah said. "Strangely, nobody felt like having anything to eat. Cook threw away the rest of that soup in the cold room. Everyone's very nervous."

"Who do you think could have done such a thing?" Mary asked, keen to know what Hannah had learned, because it was very likely that the household staff, though refraining from eating, must have been talking about it nonstop.

"I don't know, but I heard a few people say that on his last visit here, which was a few weeks ago, shortly before we arrived, Hugh was very bullying and nasty to the help."

"Really?" Pulling on her nightgown, Mary digested this interesting fact, which changed things somewhat. If Hugh had been really unpleasant to a member of the serving team, or the housemaids, then they might have decided it was payback time, now that he was here again.

And just as all the guests had known about Hugh's preference for celery soup, she remembered that the valet had come back and told her which soup it would be, in front of all the kitchen staff.

So almost everyone in Drakeley Castle had known that Hugh Barnsby-Loxton would be eating an individual serving of soup. It was practically an invitation for a poisoner to step forward and do the deed, Mary thought worriedly.

No wonder it was necessary to whisper!

One of the staff themselves might be keeping their eyes and ears wide open to make sure nobody found out.

And Mary knew well that a person who had killed once, could kill again.

She wished she knew more – so that she'd know who to avoid at mealtimes.

"Do you have any more details on that?" she asked. "Do you know who he was particularly rude to?"

"I don't as yet," Hannah admitted. "I wasn't talking much, what with sitting and worrying about you, so I didn't ask. But tomorrow, I can ask. There's bound to be a lot of information circulating. I'll pick up as much of it as I can."

"So will I," Mary said.

She hadn't thought she'd get a wink of sleep, what with everything that had happened that night, the unfair accusation from Duchess Drakeley, and worst of all, the expression she'd seen in Gilbert's eyes.

However, she was utterly exhausted after her long day's work. It seemed that she'd only closed her eyes for a moment before the knock on their door, from a passing footman, signaled that it was morning, and time for them to report for work again.

Mary sat up in bed, turning on the light and giving an enormous yawn. She still felt shattered, and those couple of hours of sleep hadn't made a dent in her tiredness. Her eyes felt full of prickly dust, and she was bone-weary in a way she hadn't been since first starting work at the factory.

She had coped with that – the hardest challenge of her life. And she'd cope with this. Reminding herself that she was tough and strong and had managed to deal with life's harshest challenges so far, Mary climbed out of bed, wincing as her bare feet hit the cold floor.

Quickly, she and Hannah dressed, and then they hurried out of their room, joining the corridor that led to the kitchens.

At this hour, the only people who were up and about were the servants. After such a long, taxing night, Mary was sure the guests would only rise much later.

But as she headed into the kitchen, she realized that her working day was not going to be as straightforward as she thought. On seeing her arrive, the cook spun around, distracted from the pot of water she was bringing to the boil for the oats, and staring at Mary in consternation.

"Oh, dear – Miss Adams. I – I thought you were going to be arrested!"

Was that a trace of doubt and fear in Mrs. Waddington's good-natured face? With a pang, Mary remembered this was what murder did. The terrible deed sowed suspicion and distrust among people.

"The constable looked at the evidence and decided there were a lot of others who might be responsible," she said politely.

"But nobody else has been arrested as yet?" The cook's eyes were even wider now.

"Not as yet, I believe."

The cook let out a stressed sigh. "Well, I'm afraid we're going to have to put you on duty elsewhere. We can't have you in working with the food, young lady. Even if you're as pure as – as the driven snow, there hasn't been anyone else brought in as yet, and as a result, nobody will eat a bite if they know you've set foot in the kitchen!"

As if she was doing a painful but necessary task, she strode over to Mary, grasped her shoulders, and gently turned her around, marching her out of the kitchen until she was beyond the doorway.

"That's as close as you come," she said firmly. "You must eat your meals elsewhere – in your room will probably be the best place. I'll see you get a good breakfast and lunch, don't worry. And now, go and report to the housekeeper, and see what work she can find for you."

Feeling like a pariah, but understanding that the cook was only doing what she had to do, Mary nodded. She turned and walked away guessing that at this hour, the housekeeper would be busy in the parlor or the drawing room, directing her team to anything that needed attention after the previous night, and distributing the room cleaning schedule.

That might mean, if she was on room cleaning duty, that she'd have a chance to see Gilbert again. She was desperate to speak to him after what had happened last night. Of all the people in Drakeley Castle, he was the one who needed to believe she was innocent, but the Drakeleys might have convinced him otherwise.

She had to find him somehow – and time was ticking by.

If he left the castle without Mary having the chance to explain herself, she worried there was a strong chance she'd never see him again.

CHAPTER SIXTEEN

Mary's first guess about the housekeeper's whereabouts was right. Before she reached the parlor, she heard Miss Hobbs' voice, loud and brisk, allocating duties.

"You'll be on glassware and silverware today, Miss Scott, and you'll be responsible for stripping all the beds as soon as the guests leave, Miss Davis."

When Mary walked in, Miss Hobbs fell briefly silent.

She stared at Mary with the selfsame consternation she'd seen on the cook's face. Nobody wanted anything to do with her this morning, that was clear. Nobody!

"Good heavens," the housekeeper said abruptly. "What are you doing here, Miss Adams?"

"The police are still investigating," Mary said, repeating a story she was getting tired of telling, because it didn't help to erase that suspicious frown from anybody's face. "So, for now, I'm reporting for duty. The cook said it will be better if I don't work in the kitchens today."

The housekeeper shook her head. "I can't have you in front of the guests at all. They'll be very upset. This whole situation is extremely disturbing!" It was very clear that she thought it was somehow Mary's fault. "I think you'll need to be on laundry duty today. Go and report to the laundry house. We've got Miss Hereford working there, and she'll be grateful for some help. There's a mountain of sheets and blankets that'll be coming through for washing today, so you'll be busy." Her voice dropped. "Just please – please keep out of everybody's way, will you?"

"Yes, ma'am," Mary agreed, gritting her teeth at the unfairness of it all. Even Constable Philpott acknowledged that the killer might be lurking elsewhere in Drakeley Castle. If she was still a strong suspect, he'd have locked her away. But it didn't seem to make a difference to anyone's mindset.

In their opinion, she was a guilty woman who was now looking for the first available chance to poison somebody else!

How patently ridiculous was that?

But, trailing away, Mary knew that in this environment of fear and distrust, she was lucky to have a job to do at all, and not to be confined to her bedroom room for the day. That would have been terrible, festering in her worried thoughts in that icy room.

The advantages of doing laundry were that she'd spend all day in healthy physical activity, doing a constructive job. And thanks to the steamy temperatures of the boiler, she'd be in the only really warm part of the castle on this particularly icy and windy morning.

Trying to see the bright side as clearly as she could, Mary hurried out of the side door and along the short walkway to the outside room, with its water pipes and giant boiler, and another section near the boiler where clothes could be hung, to dry quicker in the warmth.

Although many items had to be washed by hand, Castle Drakeley had two small but efficient washing machines, which bounced and rattled their way through the wash cycle, meaning that a lot of the arduous labor of bygone days, was no longer necessary.

"Good morning, I'm here to help today," she said, walking into the basement room and immediately feeling her skin start to thaw in the humid, steamy air.

Miss Hereford, who Mary knew by her first name of Barbara, was bent over one of the machines, stacking clothes inside. Upon hearing Mary's voice, she uttered a little shriek and spun around, staring at Mary in consternation, the same way she might stare at a large rat that had poked its whiskery nose into the laundry room.

"You!" she said, and then, as if remembering her manners too late, she added, "Er, I mean, I was just startled, that's all."

But the way she was looking at Mary, 'just startled' was clearly not the real reason for her sudden fright.

"Don't worry," Mary said, suddenly tired of being unfairly suspected, and running out of patience with this entire scenario. "I don't have any poison on me, and in any case, there's no food around."

Barbara let out a nervous giggle, shifting from foot to foot as Mary sighed.

"You don't honestly think I did this? With me being about the only person who didn't know Hugh Barnsby-Loxton?"

"I guess so," Barbara admitted. "I'm sorry for acting that way. I think we're all a bit nervy right now."

"Well, if you feel bad, think how I feel being wrongly suspected," Mary pointed out. "It's frankly awful, and if everyone keeps believing it, then the real killer will never be found."

"That's also true." But now, Barbara's demeanor had relaxed.

Moving over to the large laundry basket, Mary began sorting the clothes and bedding, separating the whites from the darks, and the delicate fabrics from those that would withstand a brisk machine wash.

"I understand that he was rude to some of the staff last time he was here?" Mary asked as she worked. Perhaps her session in the laundry room might allow her to pick up some valuable information.

"He's always rude to everyone," Barbara admitted. "I have friends who work at their manor house – it's an enormous place. They try to keep out of his way, because they never know if they'll get the sharp side of his tongue on a bad day," she admitted. "I suppose they won't need to do that anymore, though."

"Did anyone here have a particular problem with him? I mean, any of us – the maids, the butlers?"

But Barbara shrugged. "Ain't it always the way?" she said philosophically. "He's not the only rude guest we've had to deal with. There's always plenty of those. But I can't think of any one of us who would have been upset enough to do – well, to do something like that. I mean, it's life in prison at best. Most likely, hanging. All for the sake of revenge 'cause someone was rude? It doesn't make sense to me," she admitted.

Nor did it to Mary. But she remembered that Hannah would also be asking questions, and that she might get a different insight. Perhaps there were secrets to be uncovered in this castle, and a darker motive might have been carefully concealed by one of the staff, who'd waited until the time was right.

"Oh, dear," Barbara said. "I see we're out of soap. I meant to go and get some more on the way in, but – well, with everything going on, I've been a bit distracted," she said apologetically.

"I'll go. Is it in the storeroom above the cellar?" Mary asked. She didn't mind venturing out into the cold for a brisk walk. The storeroom above the cellar was nowhere near the kitchens, so nobody could accuse her of coming in for nefarious reasons.

"Yes, it's there," Barbara said.

"I'll be a minute."

Mary headed out of the warm laundry room, unrolling her sleeves and pushing them all the way down her arms again as she crossed the paved walkway, which was in the teeth of a ferocious wind. The sky was a vivid blue, as if it was completely innocent of the freezing temperatures that had set in, and just trying to do its best by providing some sunshine.

Of course, Mary had an ulterior motive for going to get the soap. Being confined to the laundry room for the day meant that this might be her only chance to see Gilbert again. He might even be leaving this morning, since he'd been here specifically for the disastrous engagement party, and would probably want to use this fine weather for the drive up north.

She didn't want him to go without getting the chance to make things right. If only to say a quick goodbye and try to clear the air between them. Last night had ended on such a disastrous note, and she desperately wanted to smooth things over – even if, to use a laundry analogy, she wasn't sure how crumpled they might be.

Because of this, she bypassed the storage room and continued down the corridor, listening out hard for any footsteps that might be coming her way, and taking note of any bolt holes she could use to duck away and hide.

There were no footsteps. The hour was still early, and it seemed that most of the guests were still in the safety of their bedrooms. That meant she would need to knock on Gilbert's door.

If that was what it took to see him, then that was what she would do.

But, as she passed the parlor, Mary saw that it was not empty, and that there was one guest inside, sitting at the tidy, and freshly polished table, and sipping on a cup of tea.

She couldn't help a guilty startle as she saw him there, and of course, his own head swung around.

It was the mystery man from yesterday, the one who'd arrived here for a reason she still didn't know about – Mr. Everington.

"Good morning, Miss Adams," he said in measured tones that contained not a little wariness. Mary felt herself flush. She should have known that somebody, at least, would be up and about at this hour. In her anxiety and determination to see Gilbert, she'd overlooked the reasonable likelihood of that happening.

Far too optimistic as always, she chastised herself.

"Good morning, sir," she replied. Then, wanting to seem helpful, she added, "I'm not on serving duty today, but if there's anything you need, I'll fetch it for you, or ask one of the other maids."

"I'm well taken care of," he said, setting down his cup and picking up an oat biscuit. He took a very deliberate bite of it, as if showing her that he wasn't scared to be eating in front of her.

Mary noted, though, that it was a very small bite. No more than a nibble.

"What a catastrophe last night turned out to be," he said in tones that now hinted at a question.

"It was a disastrous, tragic evening and I hope police find the killer as soon as possible," Mary said firmly.

He quirked an eyebrow, put his biscuit down, and picked up his cup again. "Let's hope justice takes its course," he said cryptically. "Where are you working today?"

Guessing that he was making sure she wasn't going to be in the kitchens, Mary set his mind at rest.

"I'm doing laundry today. I've just come in to get some equipment," she explained. He wasn't to know that she'd already gone past the storeroom and had another goal in mind.

He nodded, but didn't reply.

Deciding that this very strange conversation was now over, Mary wished him a good morning, and continued on her way. She hadn't wanted to be sidetracked, even for an instant. She had limited time before she'd need to be back in the laundry room, and her goal was to find Gilbert.

Hoping that this very strange, and overly curious Mr. Everington wouldn't follow her, she headed along the corridor – past the first door, then the second one, then past the branch in the corridor where the passage headed down to the old armory. And then, the next door was Gilbert's.

She was about to knock. In fact, she'd already raised her hand to do just that.

The next moment, she snatched it away from the door as if the wood was red-hot. From inside the room, she'd heard Constable Philpott's annoyingly distinctive tone.

He was inside there, questioning Gilbert.

And Mary's face flushed deep red with stress, as she remembered that apart from Hannah, Gilbert was the only person in Drakeley Castle who knew about her involvement in not one, but two, previous murder cases.

Would this be enough to point the finger of blame directly back at her again?

She hesitated for only a moment. Yes, she felt guilty about doing it, but this was a crisis situation, she reasoned. This was her future at stake, and she needed to know.

Stepping forward as quietly as she could, Mary pressed her ear to the door.

CHAPTER SEVENTEEN

The door was thick and solid, and Mary had to adjust her stance so that her ear was as close as possible to the keyhole. That was where the best sound from inside was to be found. Now, bending over and listening hard, she could hear the actual words, rather than the sounds, of the two men inside the room.

"So, tell me, Mr. MacLeod, now that you have given your version of events," Philpott paused. Mary couldn't hear the scratching of his pen on the paper. The door was too thick for that. But she could imagine the scene – the constable probably sitting on the desk chair, since that was where he liked to be if he could, and Gilbert in the armchair. "Now that I've had that, I'd like some background. I understand you met the suspect, Mary Adams, just before the – er – incident at Coldstream Lodge, and that you have interacted with her since then?"

Gilbert would have his hair still tousled from sleep and be wearing casual trousers and a plaid shirt. Mary was sure, knowing his love for the outdoors, that he'd been planning on going for a walk before leaving. She could imagine him, striding across the frosty ground, into the teeth of the wind, a scarf wrapped around his neck, letting the icy breeze refresh him, and help to put the troubling memories of last night into perspective.

Catching herself, and reining in her imagination, Mary listened carefully as Gilbert replied. Her heart was thrumming with tension. Listening at the door like this was a recipe for disaster. Wasn't there a saying: listeners never hear any good of themselves? She was sure she'd heard something like that, while at school, and she could understand the truth of it. Gilbert was in a difficult predicament right now, talking to an officer of the law. Of course, he would tell him everything he knew! And since Mary was sneakily listening in, she had to be prepared for him to say some unpalatable things about her. In fact, this could be where their friendship ended.

The thought made her swallow hard. But it didn't stop her leaning even closer, placing her ear right on the cold steel of the lock, as he replied.

"I've known Mary Adams ever since that time, yes. I believe I met her on her first day of work at Coldstream Lodge, but I departed the lodge before the – the incident you refer to." He paused. "And then, while I was at Middlefield Manor, there was another unfortunate murder."

"And Miss Adams was once again a suspect?" Mary shuddered. The constable now sounded as if he was on the hunt. He was clearly regretting having agreed to let her out of that small study last night.

"Miss Adams was not a suspect, and in fact, she was the one who pursued the idea it was murder. If it hadn't been for her efforts, the killer would never have been found, and the death deemed accidental," Gilbert said firmly. "She is a woman of a fine, ethical character."

Listening to him standing up for her, Mary felt tears prickle her eyes. Tears of relief – and another, more complex emotion.

"That's interesting. I'll certainly check that version of events with the local constabulary," Philpott said, sounding somewhat disappointed at having had holes poked in his theory so early on.

"You know," Gilbert said, speaking in an even lower voice, so that Mary had to strain her ears, "I've had a lot of dealings with the people in these stately homes, in my travels, which have taken me all over England and Scotland. It's shocking to see what does go on sometimes, what I get told about, and what gets covered up. To me, it's not suspicious that Miss Adams should have been in three different stately homes where crimes have occurred. They happen more often than you'd think, and get covered up a lot of the time."

"Interesting." Mary was sure Philpott was now scribbling frantically as these revelations were shared.

There was a snap that made her jump. That was him, closing the notebook with an air of finality, she realized, quickly backing away from the door. She turned and, on silent feet, ducked down the corridor in the direction of the old armory, pressing herself behind a pillar in the wall so that the constable wouldn't see her as he left.

Gilbert's door opened. The constable's footsteps headed down the passage. He knocked on the next door, and a moment later, it opened and closed.

That meant she had an opportunity – and there was no time to waste.

Mary rushed back down the passage and tapped softly on Gilbert's door.

"C'min," he said casually. From his tone, she could tell he thought it was the constable again, making a return visit, possibly to ask Gilbert if he was sure about Mary's character, or if he'd changed his mind about her.

She opened the door and tiptoed inside.

Gilbert was sitting in the armchair, with his hands laced behind his tousled head, and he was wearing casual trousers and a plaid shirt, and he did have his walking boots on. She'd been right on all counts, Mary thought, astonished by how accurately she'd visualized the scene.

But she hadn't anticipated how Gilbert's demeanor would change when he saw her.

His casualness vanished. He sat bolt upright. His hands clasped each other tightly in front of him, and he stared at Mary with a look of distinct dubiousness in his eyes.

Quickly, feeling shocked by what she was seeing, Mary explained her reason for being here.

"I wanted to speak to you after – after what happened last night," she said in a soft voice. "It was all so disturbing, and so many people suspect me."

That was his cue to say he didn't suspect her. But Gilbert missed his cue. His frown deepened as he stared at her, and Mary's stomach twisted.

"You know, I happened to overhear a conversation yesterday night," he said.

A sense of doom settled inside her.

"What – what conversation was that?"

"It was a conversation between Lady Diana and a man – I'm not sure who he was, as I didn't recognize the voice. Nor did I try to listen, but as I passed the door, I hesitated, because it didn't make sense. Diana was saying, 'We can get married now,' and the man was saying, 'Yes, we can.'"

He drew in a deep breath and stared at her.

"I would never speak badly of you or your character. But I heard Diana last night, defending you to the hilt. And then, I heard that conversation. And it has me worried, Mary – thinking about how far you might have gone to help a friend in need."

Mary goggled at him. Shock was thrumming through her. Gilbert had put two and two together – two perfectly reasonable numbers – and he'd come up with a reasonable sum total. The problem was it was totally wrong – but it could have been right! If Mary was a different character, perhaps she would have considered doing just what Gilbert suspected her of.

She couldn't even feel offended, because in the last place she'd worked, when a murder had occurred, she'd briefly suspected Gilbert. Now, the tables were turned.

"I know," she said. "Diana told me how miserable she was to be marrying Hugh, and that she felt powerless, and there was nothing she could do, because her family needed the money. But I didn't poison Hugh, and nor would I have done that," she said.

"Are you sure?" Gilbert looked dubious.

"I don't even know how poison works!" Mary said, spreading her hands in a gesture of innocence. "I've spent the last three years of my life in a factory making engines. I haven't a clue how one would even get hold of poison, never mind use it! And – well, to me it would be far too risky. What if somebody innocent had died because they put the wrong bowl in front of the wrong person? What if I'd had a taste of that soup to check the seasoning before plating it up?" Her breath came faster as she voiced that horrible thought.

Gilbert's eyes widened. That was clearly an eventuality he had not considered.

"I guess what you say is true," he said. "I'm just having difficulty with the fact that you have been at three manor houses, where three separate deadly incidents have played out. I know it's probably not your fault, but it's still – well, disturbing."

He was being totally honest with her, and she had no choice but to be just as honest in return.

"Nobody's more disturbed by it than me!" she defended herself. "It's awful! All I want is to live a peaceful life and focus on building my nest egg of savings so that I can better myself one day. I keep on moving jobs because of all this happening. And that's very disruptive. I just wish that people who lived and worked in these big houses weren't so – so murderous," she said, remembering his earlier words to Constable Philpott that she'd overheard.

Gilbert nodded. "It seems they are murderous," he agreed. "And I apologize for suspecting you. I wish things were different. A quiet life would be good."

"Finding the killer would be good," Mary said firmly. She turned to the door, addressing him over her shoulder as she left. "I'm going to look into this crime myself, and solve it. Because when it comes to – to people suspecting me who I really like – well, it leaves me no choice."

"Mary! Wait!"

But having got that off her chest – and let him know what was in her heart, she didn't want to wait any longer in that room.

She turned the handle, stepped out, closed it behind herself, and then headed back down the corridor as fast as she could.

Her quest for soap had already taken far too long, and she needed to get back to the laundry. But, as she headed back to the store room, she realized that the time for roaming around the house unobserved was definitely up. People were starting to leave their rooms, and the manor house was waking.

Walking toward her, and eyeing her with a piercing gaze, was none other than Cameron Pratt, Hugh's neighbor and best friend, and the person who was surely going to be the most furious, and enraged, about his death.

Seeing Gilbert again might just have landed her in more trouble than she was ready for.

CHAPTER EIGHTEEN

Mary set her expression in a mask of calm innocence as Cameron approached. She reminded herself that she knew she was innocent. It was just everyone else – or most of them – that still believed she'd poisoned Hugh Barnsby-Loxton for some unfathomable reason.

"Well, look who's here," Cameron said under his breath as he approached her. He was clearly not going to hold back. "It's the killer maid. Why did you do it, sweetie? Did you just not like the look of him, or were you experimenting with toxic herbal ingredients? Being a humble little kitchen maid, and all that?"

The words stung, and so too did the tone in which they were spoken. Cameron was going out of his way to be hurtful, and he was stooping straight to personal insults. It was almost as if he was getting a vindictive joy in accusing her of the crime. What a nasty person he was! He seemed more gleeful about taunting her than he was upset about his friend.

"Good morning, sir," she said politely, every muscle in her face quivering to hold that serene mask in place.

Although she didn't look directly at him as she passed, she heard him give an annoyed sigh, as if he was upset that his baiting hadn't had any visible result.

And then, she was past, quivering all over.

After that, she was more than ready to grab the soap from the store room, and head straight back, to do laundry, and work her angst out in honest hard labor for a few warm, steamy hours.

She hurried to the store room, took the soap from off the shelf, and headed back at a run.

"Oh, there you are!" Turning around from her hand-washing bowl, Barbara looked relieved as Mary hurried back into the laundry room, set the soap down, and rolled her own sleeves up. "I was beginning to think something had happened to you – you know, with all this trouble. I was wondering if I should fetch it myself."

"I'm sorry for taking so long. There was someone I wanted to speak to quickly, and this was my only chance," Mary explained.

Barbara's eyes widened in evident curiosity, but Mary wasn't saying another thing.

She shook a scoop of soap into a tub, added warm water, and took a few items from the hand washing pile, immersing herself in the activity and making sure that every garment was as squeaky clean as she could get it.

Meanwhile, her mind was racing with ideas and theories and going back over the conversations she'd had. Sometimes, when you replayed things in your mind, theories became very obvious to you that had seemed less so at the time.

Mary was forming such a theory now. And once she'd thought of it, it wouldn't go away.

Harsh and unpalatable as it was, she had to acknowledge it might be the truth.

***

"Is that the time?" Barbara's words distracted her from her task of wringing out a large pile of lacy petticoats. "We'd better go and get some lunch, hadn't we?"

Realizing that despite the tension of her circumstances, she was starving, Mary almost agreed. And then, just in time, she remembered that she was banned from the kitchen and not allowed to set foot inside it.

"I'll take lunch in my room," she said. "It's what I agreed on with – with the cook and the housekeeper."

Barbara was already nodding knowledgeably, clearly seeing why Mary's absence from the dining quarters had been insisted on.

"You need me to bring you anything?" she asked kindly.

"I shouldn't think so. I'm sure they'll have remembered, but thank you," Mary said.

They left the laundry room and went their separate ways – Barbara to the staff tearoom, and Mary down the stairs to her basement room.

The door was open, and she saw with a skip of her heart that Hannah was inside.

Her friend was sitting cross-legged on her bed, drinking a cup of tea. And a tray loaded with luncheon food was on the small table between their beds.

"I was hoping you'd get some time off round about now," Hannah said. "Go on, tuck in."

"This is so kind of you," Mary said, grateful for her friend's support, and for the slices of pork pie, raisin bread, and apple tart that were piled on the tray. Taking a slice of pork pie, she realized she was so hungry she was shaking. Yesterday, there hadn't been much time for eating – before or after the catastrophe.

"I've been asking around," Hannah said in a low voice. "I've had the opportunity to talk to a lot of the maids. Almost everyone, in fact."

"What are they saying?" Mary asked, in the same low voice. This information could prove crucial.

"They all hated Hugh and considered him to be a right rude oaf," Hannah said bluntly. "But as for murdering him, I don't think anyone hated him that badly. You know, they're all good people here in service at Castle Drakeley. And it wasn't like he lived here, he just visited occasionally. No reason to go harming him, but rather just to be glad to see the back of him."

Taking a slice of apple tart, Mary decided this fitted in with what Barbara had said. They were looking for a nonexistent killer among the staff, because nobody's motive was strong enough.

"One thing I did learn is that 'most everyone was in the kitchen before dinner," Hannah said. "All the guests, I mean. Everyone saw somebody different there. One came in to get a biscuit, another came in to top up a teapot, another came in to ask one of the maids to clean up some spilled wine, and at least one came to steal a sausage. You know, it was all a bit chaotic and they didn't have enough maids and butlers on duty in the drawing room, what with all the food preparation. So people drifted through. I think they were quite curious, seeing as how the kitchen's so close by the dining room. All those smells lured them in. The only person who wasn't there, and couldn't have done it, is that strange man Lucas Everington, who arrived so suddenly."

"So he wasn't in the kitchen?" Mary had been harboring her suspicions about his timely arrival at the castle, but now it looked like he could not have committed the crime.

"Definitely not. I know for sure, because people were talking about him, and wondering where he's from. Everyone's puzzled about why he's here, but even Hugh's own servants say that he and Lucas didn't know each other at all," Hannah said.

"Then one of the others, who is not Lucas Everington," Mary said firmly, "took advantage of all that chaos to poison the soup."

"I think that's what must have happened," Hannah agreed. "But how on earth are we going to find out who?"

"I have an idea," Mary told her. She reached for a slice of thickly buttered raisin bread and took a last swallow of tea before setting the cup down. "It's not a nice idea. I don't want to be thinking the way I am. But seeing I only have a half-hour for lunch, I want to spend the rest of it looking for this person. And asking her, to her face, if she's the killer."

Seeing Hannah's eyes widen, Mary set her cup down and stood up. Bread in hand, she headed out. Time was ticking by, she had a killer to find – and now she needed to figure out where in this vast, chilly castle, Diana Drakeley would be.

Most people were now out of their rooms, and either in the dining room, or in the parlor. One or two were leaving. Cars were departing, and butlers were ferrying belongings along the corridors and out of the front door.

With so much activity, Mary hoped there would be a better chance of mingling in and going unnoticed. She bundled her hair up under her cap so that none of those distinctive locks could be seen. Hiding her hair would give her a better chance of quickly going past the rooms, glancing in, seeing if she could see or hear Diana anywhere.

She wasn't in the parlor. She wasn't in the dining room, and to Mary's surprise, she also wasn't in her bedroom.

Where was she? Scenarios spun through her mind as she considered what Diana might have done and where she might be by now if she was guilty.

It was only by chance, passing by a first-floor window, that she glanced out at the rose garden, which was a secluded spot, green and leafy, guarded by high topiary hedges, with paths crisscrossing the garden's interior, and the first buds starting to appear on the roses.

She was there! Swathed in a big jacket, with a woolen hat on her head, looking cold and restless, and pacing to and fro along one of the paths.

Deeply relieved that she'd spotted her, Mary rushed to the nearest exit point, which was the large wooden door on the far side of the armory.

She pushed it open after a brief struggle, and as she stepped out, remembered that this conversation would need to be quick, because she wasn't technically supposed to be outside the castle at all. And the rose garden was most definitely outside its thick stone walls.

Rushing there, she agonized over the best way to approach this very delicate issue. After all, Diana was her friend. And she'd stood up for her, explained that she had no motive, and done her best to persuade her parents that Mary should be released from the freezing imprisonment in the small study. Now, she was going to point a finger at her and call her a killer?

It was a most uneasy situation. And, as she reached the rose garden, seeing Diana look around in surprise, Mary hadn't the faintest idea how to broach this potentially explosive topic.

"Mary! I've been wondering where you were," Diana said, and she picked up an uneasy note in her voice. "I've been worrying about you and hoping you're feeling all right after yesterday."

"I'm not feeling all right," Mary admitted, "and everyone still thinks I'm the killer."

"Well," Diana said, still with that note of uncertainty in her voice, "I don't."

There was no more opportunity to tiptoe around the topic, Mary decided. If she tried to approach this politely, she'd be here all day!

Firstly, she didn't have all day, because if Constable Philpott saw her, he'd probably bring her into the police station and lock her away for defying his orders.

And secondly, Diana was clearly out here for a reason, and Mary strongly suspected she was waiting for her beloved in this secluded spot, and if he arrived, then the time for questioning would be over.

Knowing her words were likely to cause shock, she blurted them out regardless.

"Is that because you're the killer?" she asked, trying to achieve a politely conversational tone, to lessen their harshness. She drew a deep breath, waiting for the repercussions she knew would come.

CHAPTER NINETEEN

"What?" Diana drew herself up to her full height, spitting out the word as Mary flinched away. For a moment, all her aristocratic lineage shone through as she looked both beautiful and furious. Her eyes blazed. Her slender fingers clenched together. Mary thought she might have stamped her foot. At any rate, there was a scuff of gravel.

"You're calling me a killer! Me? After all I've been through?"

The friendliness had vanished from her voice – temporarily, Mary hoped.

"You haven't really been through anything," she reasoned. "Hugh Barnsby-Loxton died after you'd been engaged for approximately five seconds. I don't believe that's long enough to cause undue suffering."

"But – it was all the suffering leading up to it that I had to endure!" Diana protested. "Plus, there was the extreme mental angst of knowing that I was going to meet with my parents today and tell them that I was calling the engagement off."

"What?" Mary said, shocked. "You were going to do that?"

Diana sighed. She'd never been good at holding a grudge, Mary remembered, from the conversations they'd had. And now, her brief flare of fury was evaporating as fast as it had come.

"I didn't want to tell you, the night before last, when I came to see you," she admitted. "So I guess there's a reason why you might think I – I'd done such an awful thing. But I realized there was no need to when I could call the engagement off." She shivered. "I'm going to catch my death out here, and so are you. Can we at least walk up and down to keep warm?"

They began to tread along the gravel paths, feet scrunching, moving from one hedge to the other.

Mary frowned as she thought about her words.

"You didn't call the engagement off. It happened. It was announced which is why the Barnsby-Loxtons were doubly furious. Not only did they lose their son, but they also had to contractually hand over a hundred acres of land."

Diana looked at the gravel in front of her, speeding up the pace of her walk.

"This is a difficult thing to say," she said eventually. "But I studied that whole agreement for hours, back to front and inside out. There was nothing in it at all that prevented me calling the engagement off." Anger resounded in her voice again. "It was as if whichever solicitor drafted it, didn't think for a moment that a woman would possess a will of her own, and choose to do something different! And nor did it say anywhere, that if I called the engagement off, the land would revert to the Barnsby-Loxtons."

Mary nearly choked as she realized the implications of Diana's actions.

Her sneaky friend had found a contractual loophole that would have allowed her family to benefit from the hundred acres, while then ensuring that she didn't have to marry the obnoxious Hugh. Mary felt a serious level of admiration for the contrariness it would have taken to make such a bold and brilliant move.

"So, as you can see," Diana said, "there was no reason at all for me to need to murder anyone. I had it all planned out, and was going to call the engagement off at breakfast, and announce my engagement to the man I love at lunch. I thought a few hours' delay would probably be polite, and by then with any luck, the Barnsby-Loxtons would have left. I was as surprised as anybody when he dropped down dead, and I didn't need to do any of that after all," she confided.

Mary heard only truthfulness in her tone.

And her plan had been flawless, with the added benefit that there were no dead bodies or policemen involved.

"I see now I was wrong," she admitted.

"It's really no problem. I was angry that you'd think of me that way – but I suppose, since somebody clearly did murder Hugh, we're all entitled to have our suspicions." Diana checked the time on her watch, pushing back her jacket sleeve.

"Are you waiting for your fiancé-to-be?" Mary asked.

"I am. He said he'd have a quick word with me out here, a final goodbye before he departs. After last night, we rethought our plans, and decided it will be best to wait a few more weeks before we make the announcement," she said.

Really?

A new, dark suspicion was now forming in Mary's mind.

"Your fiancé, who is he?" she asked innocently. Then, as Diana hesitated, she added, "You can tell me because I'm going to have to get back to work any minute. I'd just like to know, though – so I know."

Diana leaned forward. She whispered in Mary's ear, "His name's Harold Burbridge. Doesn't that sound lovely? Diana Burbridge is who I'll become, this summer. He doesn't have a fortune, but I don't care! We'll have each other, and that's enough."

Mary gave her hand a squeeze, but the suspicions were now crowding her mind.

She remembered who Harold was. She'd heard someone say his name at the dinner table when she'd brought the soup in. He was a man of about thirty, who'd been wearing a gray jacket and tie, with a broad, pleasant face and a genial laugh.

Harold Burbridge might not have money.

But by marrying Diana, he'd stand to gain more money than he'd had, especially with that hundred acres.

Maybe Harold hadn't wanted to risk it and had decided to take matters into his own hands to be absolutely sure that Hugh was out of the picture.

Heading back into the castle, slamming the wooden door shut behind her and hurrying through the armory, Mary further reasoned that Harold might not even be waiting around to say goodbye to Diana. What with the police knocking on doors, and suspects being ruled out, and Mary herself having been at least temporarily cleared, maybe Drakeley Castle was starting to feel like a threatening place.

A place he might be better off leaving without saying goodbye to anybody.

Looking for him could land her in big trouble. The garages were even further away from the castle than the rose garden was, and with people coming and going, there was a bigger chance she might be seen.

She would know him immediately if she saw him again, she thought, heading for the garages, and hoping she could get there without anyone shouting her name.

The garages were a large, stone outbuilding that was a good five-minute walk from the castle itself. The building served a double purpose as a store room for machinery and tools, as well as having a large, clear space at the front where visitors could park.

Most of the guests had drivers or valets, and the drivers or valets would fetch the cars and bring them to the castle doors. But Harold, being less wealthy, would have driven himself, without the help of servants.

As soon as Mary burst through the large double doorway, she realized she was right.

The rattle of an engine was loud in the silence. A modest black Ford at the end of the row of luxury cars had its engine running, warming up while its driver was bent over the car's trunk, packing in a suitcase and a heavy jacket. She thought it was the same man, with that solid looking build.

"Mr. Burbridge!" she called out. "Mr. Burbridge!"

At the sound of his name, he spun around immediately, and as he saw her, the expression on his face turned even more furtive and worried than it had been.

And he'd *already* looked furtive and worried. There was something up that was clear.

"May I speak to you? I'm Mary Adams," she said, hurrying forward.

"Yes, I know who you are! I – er – unfortunately I don't have time to speak to you!"

Instead of approaching her, Harold was retreating fast. He hastily slammed the trunk, and then moved swiftly around to the other side of the car and stood there, eyeing her out with a distinct air of nervousness.

The car was between him and her.

"I need to ask you something," she said.

"Go away!" In his fright, he was flapping his hands at her, making shooing motions, as if that might somehow waft her away. Well, bad luck for Harold. All the wishful thinking and flapping gestures weren't going to work, and she was going to demand the truth from him.

She moved around the car. Harold scurried the other way, keeping diametrically opposite her.

Mary tried going the other way, and Harold, too, changed direction.

This was getting ridiculous. He was refusing to answer her questions, and now he was using the car as a metal shield to be sure she couldn't reach him. And worst of all, she didn't have time. Her lunch break was long over, and she should be back in the laundry room by now.

She should not be outside the castle walls, in the garage.

"Why are you so scared of me?" she asked.

"I'm not scared! I'm just in a big hurry, and prefer not to talk to a suspected killer"

"I'm not a killer, and you know it!"

"I never said you were! I said you were suspected. Now, I just need to leave!"

Seeing his chance, as his circling around the car took him to the driver's door, Harold wrenched it open and jumped inside, slamming it behind him.

The car's engine rose to a shrill roar, and she heard the grinding of gears as Harold, in his panic, fought to get the vehicle into reverse.

Taking advantage of the situation, with the man-against-machine struggle that was playing out here, Mary opened the passenger door, jumped in, and slammed it behind her.

"Now will you talk to me?' she demanded, hoping that she hadn't jumped from the frying pan into the fire. If Harold was prone to tipping over into a killing rage, her actions might well have triggered it.

CHAPTER TWENTY

Harold turned to stare at Mary, appalled to find her in the passenger seat of his Ford. In his confusion, his foot slipped off the pedal, and the car stalled.

"What – what on earth is this about?" he stammered, his eye twitching noticeably.

"This is childish," Mary said. "I was told you're a good person. I'm not seeing that right now. Why are you so desperate to get away, and why are you so terrified of a few simple questions."

"The police have questioned me enough," Harold mumbled, but her words caused him to redden, and she guessed he was now thinking exactly how pointless, and how incriminating, his actions had been.

"Alright. I can spare a minute. What do you want to know?" he asked, with a sigh of defeat.

"Well, for a start," Mary said, righteous indignation surging, "you do know Diana is waiting for you in the rose garden?"

She hadn't thought his face could get any redder, but it darkened to a purplish color as he gaped at her.

"Diana?" he said in a quivering voice. "You – you know?"

"I know," Mary said.

"Who else knows?" He asked the question in hushed tones that wobbled audibly.

Mary was sure that Diana's beloved had many admirable qualities, but she didn't think that reckless courage was one of them. He looked scared to death that she, and others, might know.

Unfortunately, this behavior was making her rethink his validity as a suspect. Would he have possessed the nerve to kill? Staring at his shaking hands, she was starting to have her doubts.

"Well, everybody will know if I tell them," she said. "But maybe there won't be a necessity for that. I want to know if you were the person who poisoned Hugh Barnsby-Loxton."

He stared at her, and for a moment, as she spoke the name, she saw a flash of loathing in his eyes so intense that it changed her mind. In that instant, she believed that she might have been wrong, and that he did hate the man enough to have wanted him not just out of the picture, but out of Diana's future forever.

"He was a nasty man," he said in a rush. "He was a braggart and a terrible liar, and he treated people appallingly. It filled me with despair that he was going to marry Diana." Gripping the wheel as he spoke, he left Mary in no doubt about the intensity of his feelings. But how had he acted on them?

He turned to her with a sigh.

"I'm not a fighter. I'm not an aggressive man at all. In fact, during the war, I had the most boring and non heroic job possible. I was in an office, in charge of ordinance and supplies, because I have a head for figures and I think they all knew I'd be useless on the front lines. I've always been one to avoid conflict. That was why I decided to leave now, and it was why I didn't want to engage with you. I apologize. Especially after what happened last night, I'm finding myself more averse to it than usual."

This honesty was refreshing. Yet again, within a short while, Mary found herself revising her opinion of this man. It really didn't seem like he was the killer, but she was going to reserve judgment on that for a while longer. She didn't want to make a mistake by ruling him out when he was intelligently managing to conceal his deadly agenda.

"What did you think of Hugh?" she asked. Now that he was talking freely, he might open up, and either give her more insight into him – or else, let something slip.

"I couldn't believe what an awful man he was!" Harold blustered as if he simply couldn't hold back the words and was glad to get them off his chest. "I tried not to say so in front of Diana, because after all he was her family's choice, and although I hoped that she would find it within her to break off the engagement, I didn't want to personally influence her. I mean, there was always the chance she'd end up staying with him. It was a very troubling, and tense, situation."

He sighed, rubbing a hand over his head, as if easing the brief pounding of a headache. Then he looked at her again.

"I noticed, during the evening, how disparagingly he spoke about almost everyone else. He was the only person who was brave, who was capable, who was a good character in his world. That ridiculous war story!" Harold rolled his eyes. "I heard it three times during the evening, and each time, it was more unrealistic than the last. I mean, it was obviously done with a team, but you didn't hear a word about his fellow soldiers. He was so self-obsessed!"

There was a note of intense dislike in his voice, and it made Mary prick up her ears. Harold's motive was strong.

"He was unpleasant to everybody. He was insufferably rude to his poor valet, treating him like a slave. And he wasn't only rude, but amoral."

"Amoral? In what way?" Mary asked.

Harold paused, twisting his fingers together as if wondering whether he should say what he felt. Then, with a deep, decisive breath, he continued.

"I wasn't going to mention this because it upset me too much, but you might as well know. The night before last, after dinner, he wasn't in the smoking room with the other gentlemen."

Mary nodded. She had noticed he wasn't there, and had wanted to know why, but hadn't had the opportunity to find out.

"People were asking where he was, and nobody seemed to know. The general consensus was that he'd gone to bed early. But as I retired to my room, I passed by the room of one of the female guests – not Diana. And I distinctly heard his voice coming from inside that room. He was talking to whoever it was – I have no idea who the lady was, and I didn't wait around – in a loving, soothing way. It was quite obvious what he'd been up to!" Harold said, his eyes almost popping out of his head with outrage.

"That must have made you angry?" Mary asked.

"I've heard whispers before now that this is the way he behaves. It was not a huge surprise to me. What was deeply disillusioning was that he was doing this the night before his engagement to another. It was obvious he didn't care a lot about Diana. Only that title."

"You do realize, though, that since you care for Diana, and clearly didn't want to see her marry such a horrible man, it gives you a strong motive for murder?" Mary pointed out.

There was a pause, and Harold blinked rapidly, as if only now realizing this himself.

"Yes. Yes, I suppose it would, if I'd been that person. My feeling was that if she couldn't – er – find it within herself to break off the engagement, I was going to request a meeting with her parents and explain that they were making her marry a cheater, who was only after the title. I hoped that I'd be able to get them to see sense. So yes, a bold step for me to take, as I'm not a confrontational person. But murder? Never." He frowned. "In any case, I'm not sure how I'd have done it, even if I wanted to."

"Were you in the kitchen at any time while dinner was being prepared?" Mary asked. Many of the guests had been. Was he one of them? But he shook his head decisively.

"No. Why would I go through to the kitchens in my host's home? That would be very rude. I know there was a shortage of butlers, but I'm a patient man who doesn't mind waiting until someone's available, to ask them for what I need."

That did align with his personality.

Now, at last, Mary could see that the good qualities he possessed, which had attracted Diana to him, were subtle, but they were admirable. He was a polite, considerate man, he was a person who wouldn't explode with temper but who would rather wait and reason, and he was also very observant.

At first she'd thought him to be weak and cowardly, but now she was realizing that it wasn't necessarily a positive to be a hotheaded braggart who rushed into a situation.

"If you're so innocent, then why were you leaving?" she asked. "Because despite what you've told me, getting in your car and driving away without even saying goodbye to your hopeful fiancée-to-be, is rather suspicious."

Harold considered that for a moment, frowning.

"You know, you're absolutely right about that, and I'm grateful to you for reminding me of it," he said. "I won't be leaving. I'm going to go and find Diana and head back inside so that the policeman can ask me whatever he needs to."

"You're going to do that?" Mary was surprised by this sudden turnaround.

He nodded, looking abashed. "I might hate conflict, but yes, this conversation with you has shown me I need to be brave enough to clear my name if I'm innocent. We don't have to announce our love for each other just yet, given the circumstances – but I do need to be there to support Diana."

To Mary's surprise, he climbed out of the car, pocketed his keys, and strode off in the direction of the castle.

She sat a few moments longer on the Ford's scuffed leather seat, thinking about what she'd learned. And then she, too, got out of the car. It was time to head back to the laundry room for another session with the hand wash tubs and the wringer.

But now, she had a lot more to think about.

Hugh had been involved with somebody else, while at the castle, the night before the wedding?

As she walked out of the garage into the blustery afternoon breeze, Mary caught her breath. She'd just remembered the encounter she'd had in the herb garden the morning after that.

And now, she thought she knew who that love interest was. If Mary recalled, Lady Emily been desperately upset about the rejection.

"Hell hath no fury like a woman scorned?" Mary murmured to herself as she headed briskly along the path that was a shortcut to the laundry room.

She knew who her next suspect was, and she had to find her as soon as she could.

CHAPTER TWENTY ONE

Approaching the laundry room at a run, Mary felt torn. The investigation seemed to be reaching a crucial point, and she had identified somebody with a very strong motive for killing Hugh Barnsby-Loxton. Of course, a rejected woman would be angry, and she'd want revenge.

Mary remembered well the short story, The Lady or the Tiger, which they'd studied and discussed in her last year at school. She'd found the fictional situation compelling, where a princess's lover, accused of a crime, had to choose between two doors at his trial. Behind one door was a lady of the court who the princess hated, and if he opened this door, then he'd be found innocent and she would marry him. Behind the other door was a ferocious tiger that would instantly devour him as a sign of his guilt.

Of course, the man himself had no idea which door was which – but the princess had found out – and she directed him to a door as the story ended.

Which way had she pointed him? To the lady or the tiger?

In class, they'd discussed this enthusiastically and at length, but although the lady was definitely the happier ending, Mary's personal feelings had always been that the princess, given her character, would have opted for the tiger.

Now, this rejected lover had a similar choice.

Either Lady Emily could watch her love marry somebody else – or unleash the tiger, in the form of poisoned soup, so that nobody married Hugh Barnsby-Loxton at all.

Would Lady Emily have chosen the tiger?

That was the critical question.

With a marriage theme uppermost in her mind, Mary felt wedded to this theory. She was in love with it. It made so much sense that Lady Emily would have done such a thing.

All the puzzle pieces were fitting together in a most satisfying way, until – like a shower of cold water down her back – a new realization hit Mary.

"Oh, no!"

She stopped dead as the obvious answer landed like a thunderbolt.

The lady or the tiger, though compelling, was not at all relevant in this case, because Lady Emily would have been free to kill whoever she chose. And if she was sensible and practical, she would have killed Diana!

With Diana out of her way, the obstacle to Hugh's love would have been removed.

Mary was so deep in thought as she rounded the corner, that she got a fright to see Hannah rushing toward her, on a collision course.

"Eeek!" These unpredictable circumstances had definitely made her jumpier than usual. Even Hannah was startled, stopping so suddenly that she skidded on the paving stones. Mary grabbed her hand, and Hannah quickly caught her balance.

"I came to look for you," she said. "I wanted to give you an update on what I've discovered so far. I think it's important."

"I'd love an update on the case," Mary said, "but I'm feeling very guilty about neglecting my work. Poor Barbara's been doing all the washing. So, can we talk in the laundry room, while I help her? If we talk quietly?" she said, worried about Barbara overhearing. This situation was becoming so complicated.

"I've just come from there, and Barbara's not in that room," Hannah said. "I passed by one of the bedrooms on the way here, where the housekeeper was ordering her to strip the beds. So, for now, you're the only one on duty."

"I'd like to get through at least one tub, while I talk to you about what we've found out," Mary said, feeling that this struck an acceptable balance between working and investigating.

Hurrying into the laundry room, she got the tub of hot, soapy water on the go, and readied herself for another round of hand washing – this time, a few silk blouses and some lacy underwear were the items she needed to focus on.

First things first, she needed to know if the police had made any progress.

"Do you know if Constable Philpott has identified any other suspects?" she asked, hoping that the servants would have wasted no time in sharing this news with each other if he had.

But Hannah's face fell.

"Unfortunately not," she said. "The last I heard, he was saying that everyone seems to be cleared so far, and we know what that means."

Mary exchanged a worried glance with Hannah.

She knew what that meant. It meant that Philpott was going to default to the easiest explanation, despite her lack of motive, and the good things that Gilbert had said about her. She was going to end up being the official suspect, and her stomach churned as she considered what might happen if she couldn't find the real killer in time.

"So," she said, doing her best to suppress the rising sense of panic, "where are we with the staff, then?"

"I've finished asking the staff if they know anything," Hannah said. "And I'm sure they don't. I have asked as many questions as I could. People are getting so sick of me that they start yawning when they see me coming. I'm absolutely sure none of the staff have done it themselves. But on the way, I've picked up some gossip," she added in a meaningful tone.

"What?" Mary asked, lifting and turning her washing load.

A few people have said…" She leaned forward. "They said that Hugh Barnsby-Loxton was a cheat. He was cheating on Diana already, and they weren't even married yet. Apparently he is quite the player, and has a knack for having his way with the ladies. It must be due to that excessively boring war story," she said in a puzzled way.

Mary nodded, gently rinsing and squeezing the delicate items in the soapy water.

"Yesterday, I think I bumped into a woman who desperately wanted to marry him. She was in the courtyard in tears, saying that she'd lost the love of her life. It was Lady Emily. But the problem is that I don't know if she would have been angry enough to kill him, because he rejected her. Especially when it would have been much more advantageous to kill Diana. Then she could have him after all."

But Hannah shook her head, looking deeply cynical.

"You don't have the whole story," she said.

"What is the whole story?" Carefully, Mary lifted her soapy load and deposited it in the rinsing water.

"The whole story is that before the pre-dinner drinks were served, one of the footmen saw Hugh flirting outrageously with another woman – one of the estate's neighbors. I think her name's Lady Caroline. He was asking her very suggestive questions while Lady Caroline fluttered her eyelashes and twirled her hair. And – the footman said he was doing it in front of Lady Emily. She was there, in the room. Watching."

"Well!"

The cold rinsing water felt as invigorating as Mary's thoughts.

Her theory was workable after all. Now, there was an extremely good reason why Lady Emily would have wanted to murder Hugh. Still smarting from the pain of rejection, she then had to watch while he rubbed her nose in it, by flirting with another!

If Mary's opinion of Hugh hadn't already been at rock bottom, she knew this latest piece of gossip would have landed it there. As it was, she was trying to figure out if there might be something lower than rock-bottom – because if so, it was applicable.

"I'll do one more tub of washing as quick as I can," she said. "And then, I'm going to find Lady Emily. She needs to answer some very serious questions."

"Like what?" Hannah asked, wide-eyed.

"Like where she found that poison," Mary explained darkly.

CHAPTER TWENTY TWO

Just twenty minutes later, with her conscience eased by the fact the last of the hand-washing was now done, Mary left the laundry room and headed into Castle Drakeley once more.

Where would Lady Emily be – assuming she was still here? Mary hoped she was still here. If not, she'd need to explain the situation to Constable Philpott. And, as experience had already taught her, Constable Philpott was not a good listener.

The first place she was going to look was in Lady Emily's bedroom. This would be first prize in terms of finding her, as they'd be able to have a private conversation. However, at this hour – just after lunch – it was unlikely. Her room might already have been cleaned and stripped.

Reaching the door, she tapped on it, and hearing no answer from inside, opened it to have a quick peek around.

Her suspicions were correct. The bed was stripped, and the wardrobe was empty. However, Lady Emily's suitcase was on the ottoman, so she hadn't yet left. She must be having a light lunch, and commiserating with the Drakeleys, before getting on her way.

Rushing off would have looked suspicious, Mary thought, and Lady Emily must be too clever for that. She was a sneaky woman, and she'd have to use the utmost cunning when questioning her. After all, the lady had successfully lied to Constable Philpott and convinced him she was innocent.

Most likely, she was either in the drawing room or the parlor, or possibly the castle library, but she would have to be very cautious in approaching these two places. The constable could be anywhere, she wasn't sure if the Barnsby-Loxtons had left yet, although she thought it likely – and she had no idea where Duke and Duchess Drakeley would be.

Listening at doors before she walked in would be the wisest move.

The drawing room was the closest. Sidling up to the door, she listened out for any voices coming from inside. She could hear the chink of crystal and the slosh of liquid. Somebody was having a refreshing post-lunch drink.

Abruptly, sounding very loud, she heard Duke Drakeley's voice.

"I wish this whole dratted business would be over," he said. "It's shocking that such a terrible thing occurred under our own roof. And how are we ever going to look the Barnsby-Loxtons in the eye again, or hold our heads high in their presence, when it's clear our maid poisoned their son!"

Mary bit her lip. It seemed Diana's argument hadn't been as persuasive as she'd thought. Or maybe her father had ignored it and defaulted to his own way of thinking. After all, ignoring his daughter's wishes and telling her who she was going to marry was not exactly a sign he was a good listener.

"I wonder if we should give them the hundred acres back as a gesture of goodwill." That was Duchess Drakeley speaking.

There was a sharp intake of breath from the lord. "Absolutely not! A contract is a contract, and I've already sent James there with the tractor. We can get a good spring crop of highly profitable wheat. It's just – it's just going to be very awkward until an official arrest is made."

"Hopefully, that won't be long," Duchess Drakeley said, her voice quivering with worry.

Mary turned away. It was clear from the private nature of this conversation that they were the only two in the room, and she needed to look elsewhere to locate Lady Emily.

She backtracked down the corridor and headed in the direction of the second most likely place – the parlor.

But, as she was on her way there, she heard a man's voice call out to her from one of the open doors on her right.

Guilty and worried, Mary stopped in her tracks, staring into the room.

The room was a small dining room, seldom used, which is why she hadn't thought to look inside. But at the table, with his notebook open, sat Mr. Everington.

Him again? Mary was becoming wary of his presence, and all the more so when he said, "Miss Adams. I was looking for you half an hour earlier."

Clearly, you didn't check the garage, Mary thought, wondering how long she'd be able to avoid getting noticed by the wrong people. Although, right now, she wasn't certain if this was one of the wrong people. Why did he keep on calling out to her? It really seemed as if he was taking a specific interest in her, and she had no idea why.

Could he be the killer, she wondered. His arrival here had seemed coincidental, but maybe it hadn't been. And although he hadn't seemed interested in Hugh at all, that could be a front. Maybe they were old enemies.

"Half an hour earlier, I was otherwise occupied," she said. "Is there anything you need?"

His answer nearly knocked her off her feet.

"Your mother," he said suddenly. "Her name?"

The question was so shocking it robbed Mary of words. Why on earth did this man want to know that? What possible reason could he have for asking?

"That's a very personal question," she said. She could hear the tremor in her own voice. It had been a few years since she'd last seen her mum in the hospital, but it felt like yesterday.

"I know. But there's a reason for my asking. Her name?"

"Her name was June. June Adams," Mary said.

"And your dad?"

"My dad's been dead for more than a decade!" she blurted out. "He fell off his bicycle and a bus ran him over."

"I'm really sorry to hear that. His name?" Mr. Smith asked, patiently.

"His name was Donald." Raising her chin, Mary stared him down. "I've answered a lot of very strange questions from you. I hope you don't think it rude if I ask you – what's your reason for wanting to know?"

But he shook his head, not meeting her gaze.

"I'll tell you shortly. Thank you for the information," he answered.

That was no answer at all! In frustration, Mary glared at him for a few moments, hoping the force of her stare might make him change his mind, but he bowed his head and carried on making notes, just as if she wasn't there at all.

She didn't have time to think about this perplexing situation any further, even though it was gnawing at her mind. For the time being, her goal was to find the killer. If the murderer could be arrested, it would make all other problems seem far more minor.

And she was in luck. As she approached the parlor, she could hear Lady Emily's voice. The conversation seemed one-sided, and it took Mary a moment to realize that she was on the telephone.

"Yes, I'll be leaving in the next five minutes," she said, causing Mary to shiver. She'd come very close to missing her completely. "I'll be about half an hour, and can you ask the groom to saddle up Blue Breeze? I'd like to take him out for a spin. It's such a fine day and should be light for another couple of hours."

There was a ting as she replaced the receiver, and Mary used that as her cue to walk in.

"Good afternoon, ma'am," she said politely.

Lady Emily turned and frowned. Her gaze shifted from side to side, and Mary could see that she was replaying the conversation of yesterday in her mind.

"Good afternoon," Lady Emily then said, in dismissive tones. "I don't need anything, thanks. You can call a butler to take my suitcase down."

"Actually," Mary said, hoping that this would go well and that Lady Emily wouldn't start causing a commotion, "I came to ask you something."

Deep suspicion was in Lady Emily's eyes as she stared at her.

"And what, exactly, did you want to ask?"

"Yesterday you were heartbroken, and you – you confided in me that it was due to a lost love," Mary said, trying her best to tread sensitively through this ground, which could well be studded with landmines. "That lost love was Hugh Barnsby-Loxton, wasn't it? He rejected you, and then later he flirted with somebody else in front of you and I – I just wanted to ask, how did that make you feel?"

Lady Emily's eyes widened, and her face tautened into a mask of fury. She whirled around to the mantelpiece, which contained a number of small bronze sculptures. The next moment, she'd grasped one in her hand, and before Mary could even muster her defenses, she hurled it in her direction with a yell of fury.

CHAPTER TWENTY THREE

Instinctively, Mary leaped aside, and the sculpture – of an armored knight – smashed into the wall, sending a shower of plaster down.

That could seriously have hurt her – and now, Lady Emily was reaching for another of the heavy, solid sculptures.

"Ma'am, please!" Mary begged, but with a powerful overarm throw, the lady launched it at her.

"What utter rudeness," she raged, as Mary leaped the other way. The sculpture missed her by a hair's breadth. There were several more on the mantelpiece, Lady Emily's aim seemed to be improving each time, and she was now trapped in the corner of the room. She wouldn't make it to the door in time! And she needed to keep her eye on the maddened lady.

"You are hurtful and insensitive and now you – you're implying I'm a killer! As if I would do such a thing!" she raged, sending another of the figurines hurtling in Mary's direction. It hit the window behind her and punched clean through the glass in a shower of shards.

Mary grabbed a cushion from the armchair nearby and held the plump, fringed, velvet item in front of her like a shield.

"Please! You're going to kill me if one of those hits my head!" she tried to reason, but Lady Emily was beyond reason.

"That's because you... deserve... this!" she hissed.

Eyes flashing, blond hair streaming out as she put everything into the throw, the next figurine was on a collision course with Mary's face.

Instinctively, she raised the cushion, and the figurine thudded into it, the force of the impact sending Mary staggering back.

She was going to clear the entire mantelpiece unless Mary could stop this onslaught, and the only way she could think of was to fight fire with fire.

Using her only available weapon, she raised the cushion and hurled it in Lady Emily's direction with all the force she could put behind the throw.

The cushion sailed across the room and found its perfect mark. It hit Lady Emily on the ear, as she was reaching for yet another figurine.

Her head jerked sideways, and she let out a cry of pain.

99

"Ow!" she said, dropping the figurine, which landed on her toe. "Ow!" she shrieked even louder, hopping on one leg. "That hurt! What are you doing? Stop attacking me this way!"

Capitalizing on her advantage, while the lady's focus was still derailed, Mary rushed across the room and grabbed Lady Emily's hands in hers.

"Ma'am, we need to talk," she said firmly. "And we can't talk while you keep throwing those sculptures at me!"

"Yes, we can!" Lady Emily shot back, but with both her hands in Mary's firm and strong grasp, she could tell that the lady was now arguing just for the sake of it.

"You must have been angry when you saw Mr. Barnsby-Loxton flirting with another woman," Mary said, getting the conversation back on track.

Lady Emily sighed. "I was furious," she admitted. Her shoulders slumped, and some of the rage ebbed out of her. Mary fervently hoped that enough of the anger had gone that they could now have a civil conversation. Of course, if she was the killer, then she might not have good control of her emotions, and she'd need to watch for any sudden resurgence, she warned herself.

"I was wondering if you were so furious that you might have considered poisoning him?" Mary asked, airing the difficult subject at last. "Because someone did, and it wasn't me."

"It wasn't you? Everyone seems to think it is," Lady Emily said, frowning.

"Everyone is wrong."

She shrugged – as best she could with her wrists still firmly in Mary's grasp.

"Well, it wasn't me. How would I get hold of poison? I mean, really?" She wrinkled her nose superciliously at Mary. "I can see why you're only a kitchen maid, because you're not very intelligent."

"Excuse me?" Mary shot back, indignance surging.

"I live twenty minutes away, and I arrived yesterday. Yes, I – I had an intimate moment with Hugh. To be honest, I'd partaken of too much wine," she said, tossing her mane of platinum hair again. "In a sober state, I can clearly see that he would never be husband material and was only good for a fling. But yes, at the time, marriage seemed like a good idea, and I was very distressed when he said no, he was aiming to be a duke, not a lord."

"Which gave you a motive," Mary persisted.

Lady Emily sighed. "I really am going to have to spell this out to you, aren't I? I was as mad as a wet hen, but I was here with an overnight bag, and if you recall, Hugh only flirted with that other trollop just before dinnertime. Where, exactly, was I going to have obtained poison from in that time? I don't go carrying it around with me!"

That was true. Recent experience suggested that her murder weapon of choice was more likely to be a bronze figurine.

"You're clearly trying to find someone else to blame, but accusing people who only had a reason to hate him, half an hour before he was killed, is the biggest load of nonsense I've ever heard. It's quite obvious to me that the person who did this would have planned it carefully and come prepared with the poison."

As Mary considered that bombshell, Lady Emily twisted her hands out of Mary's grasp, and flounced away.

"I'll leave you to think about that because I'm heading home now. I have a horse to ride!"

For a minute, Mary simply stood in the parlor, digesting those words, looking at the mostly empty mantelpiece, and the figurines that littered the floor opposite.

Then, thoughtfully, she went and fetched them, one by one, and put them back in their places – all except the one that had sailed through the now smashed window. She felt bad about that. She couldn't fix the glass, but she could at least draw the curtain to prevent a chilly draft rushing in through the gap.

It wasn't like she'd personally caused the breakage, but the fact remained that if Mary hadn't walked into the parlor this afternoon, that window would have been fine. With a twinge of guilt, as she tugged the curtain into place, she guessed she'd have to report the breakage when she saw Duchess Drakeley again. Already unpopular with the Drakeleys, this was going to make things even worse. But if she could find the real killer, that would go a long way toward redeeming her.

And even though she had been very unlikeable and outspokenly rude, Mary had to admit that Lady Emily had given her some very helpful insight on this mystery.

Of course, the crime could not have been committed on the spur of the moment, unless it was by somebody so evil they carried poison around with them just in case anybody angered them.

No, it was far more likely that this murder had been deliberately planned, and that Hugh Barnsby-Loxton's demise had in fact been scheduled, by the killer, for that evening because there were so many people in the castle.

Nodding wisely to herself, as she picked up the last of the figurines, Mary could clearly see where the finger of blame was now pointing, and where she needed to go next. It should have been obvious to her all along, but it had taken her a good few false starts to figure it out.

The valet, of course!

The ill-treated servant!

Her suspicions had begun with the servants, because of their proximity to the food and because of Hugh's execrable treatment of those who he considered beneath him. But although she'd ruled out the servants at Drakeley Castle, thanks to Hannah's help, she had not focused on the one servant who was closer than anybody else to the victim.

And he would have had every opportunity to poison the soup. After all, he was the one who'd requested it in the first place. He'd fussily come in and out of the kitchen, on the pretext of making sure that his employer's clearly ridiculous dietary preferences, which were nothing more than sheer bad manners and an unadventurous appetite, were indulged.

"Mr. Beamish, you had me fooled for a while – but not anymore," Mary whispered to herself, feeling a thrill of resolve as she remembered Beamish's shifty gaze, and the sideways way he'd looked at her. As the killer, he was furtive and stealthy, and she suspected that he'd have the potential for violence.

This would be a confrontation that would take all her courage. But at that moment, Mary heard a loud, sharp voice ring out from behind her.

"Miss Adams! There you are! I've been looking for you. What on earth have you been doing!"

The voice was Constable Philpott's.

CHAPTER TWENTY FOUR

Constable Philpott's unexpected arrival gave Mary such a shock that she dropped the bronze sculpture.

It landed on her foot, and just as Lady Emily had done, she let out a cry of painful surprise.

"Ow!" she squeaked, hurriedly bending down and picking it up, and then half-turning, half-hopping around to face the advancing constable.

Even all the way across the parlor, Mary could see he looked extremely angry.

"Miss Adams, you have been circulating among the guests and asking questions!" he thundered. His gaze was fixed on her, his eyes boggling with fury.

"I – er – there were just a few things I was trying to clear up. You know, just for my own personal peace of mind," she began, but he shook his head.

"You have been taking on my role, just as you did when we last met! Is this some kind of – of compulsion you have?"

"There's nothing wrong with asking a few questions," she attempted to defend herself, but the thunder of his words drowned out her admittedly feeble excuse.

"I am talking about disobeying police orders! As an officer of the law, I expect my orders to be obeyed, especially when they are issued to a strong criminal suspect!"

Mary stared at him in consternation.

"You mean you haven't found the killer yet?" she asked, appalled. "You still think it's me?"

Constable Philpott looked even angrier – something Mary hadn't thought physically possible – to be accused of not yet finding the killer.

"I have been doing my job to the best of my abilities," he seethed. "I was top of my class in my police training group, a fact I thought I already informed you of, and recently promoted to the constabulary of Little Brayshire, because of my competence! You are insinuating I've been doing nothing?" His nostrils flared. "I have ruled out almost every one of these guests. The list of remaining suspects is down to a handful of people, none of them strong suspects, none of them likely. And then, there is you! Your behavior today has convinced me of your disrespect for the law. Why should it not extend further?"

This situation was spiraling all the way out of control. And to be fair, she could see why Constable Philpott was annoyed. Mary knew that she was going to have to backtrack and fast. She didn't want to make a permanent enemy out of him, not when he was the one holding life and death powers over her future.

In her eagerness to find the killer, she had overlooked this fact. It was time to look at it again and to do what she needed to do to save the situation.

"I'm very sorry," she said.

He stared at her, lips pressed together. "Your apology is not only unconvincing, but far too late."

Nothing for it. She was going to have to reveal the direction of her suspicions.

"Look, you're right. I was asking a few questions, and ruling a few people out. But as I've been asking the questions, I've realized that there is an extremely strong suspect, and he's somebody who had the motive, and the opportunity, to commit the crime." Taking a deep breath, she continued. "You see, it was clear to me that the killer must have prepared for this moment, and come here with the poison, and the intention to murder Hugh Barnsby-Loxton while there were people around."

It hadn't been clear to her, it had been clear to Lady Emily, for whose intelligence she had newfound respect. She was a sharp lady, apart from her very poor choice in love interests.

But now, thanks to her insight, it was clear to Mary, too – and hopefully, to Constable Philpott, if he also hadn't yet figured that out.

He was frowning thoughtfully, as if this fact did indeed present a fresh insight.

"Based on that," she continued, "and on – er – the victim's poor treatment of those around him, I believe the killer must be -"

"Enough!" The word was like the crack of a whip, and Mary hastily shut her mouth. "Miss Adams, do not tell me how to do my job! The fact you are continuing to theorize about this case in a frankly unstoppable way is only eroding my trust in you. Which is already low."

If only she'd had the chance to get the name out! But right now, she couldn't say another thing. Constable Philpott was fuming at her, and he wasn't listening to her ideas.

"You're going to need to be under lock and key now, while I conclude my investigation," he decided. "I thought it was a bad idea to have you at large in this castle, and you've proven me right. Come with me."

Demonstrating his utter lack of trust in her by grasping her arm, he led Mary out of the parlor and along the corridor.

Her heart thumped hard in her chest.

This was terrible. Her efforts had been in vain, and now her fate hung in the balance. As he led her inexorably to the stairs, Mary prayed that Gilbert had already gone. She didn't want him to see her in this compromising position, especially after their last conversation, during which she'd sensed that he was conflicted about her. He'd urged the constable she was innocent – but had he himself believed it?

Mary still wasn't sure.

Although Gilbert was not in the dining room, when the constable led her past that door, the Drakeleys were, together with Cameron Pratt. Three heads turned as she passed, and the clink of forks on china was briefly silenced.

"Well, it looks as if our good constable is close to making an arrest," Duke Drakeley said in satisfied tones that rang out through the open doorway and scorched Mary's ears.

"It'll be a relief to see justice done!" Cameron added his own heartfelt – and Mary felt sure, deliberately loud – words to the conversation.

And then, they were ascending the stairs, and the constable was heading back to the one room Mary had hoped never to see again.

The small study.

"No, please! Not in there! It's icy cold!" she protested.

He shook his head. "Unfortunately, you'll have to deal with the cold for a couple of hours," he said. "If there's any consolation, Miss Adams, at least it'll make the prison cell at the Little Brayshire police station seem warm by comparison. We try to keep it at a pleasant temperature even during the winter months. We believe in humane treatment of all arrested prisoners," he said in tones that resounded with self-approval.

With that, he turned and closed the door.

A moment later, the key rattled in the lock.

Mary headed over to the armchair and collapsed down into it, burying her face in her hands.

This was the worst possible outcome.

She'd alienated Constable Philpott – a fact she realized was inevitable. He wasn't going to listen to her, and her actions had branded her a more likely criminal.

Worse still, she was now locked away in this freezing cold study while he completed his investigation, and she worried that in his mind, he was already certain who the killer now was.

Mr. Beamish! How could she find, and question, him?

Ideas spun through Mary's mind, but they all rested on somebody coming past the small study in the next few minutes, and who was going to do that? As well as being cold, the room was very remote. Hannah wouldn't come up here in the course of her work, and even if she did, would Mary really ask her friend to let her out? That would cause Hannah to be in terrible trouble.

She could ask Hannah to call Mr. Beamish, so that she could question him through the door, but with a solid door between them, and the fact she was locked away as a suspected killer herself, Mary acknowledged that she was not likely to get any answers from him. He'd just laugh at her through the closed door and walk away.

There was only one solution that might possibly save her, and it was risky in the extreme.

In order to find Mr. Beamish, question him, and clear herself, Mary was going to have to escape this room.

There was only one way to do that… and it was through the window.

The high-set, narrow window on the castle's third floor. She'd never thought of it as an option. Last night, in the dark, it had seemed like an impossible escape route. But it was light now, and she was desperate.

Was she going to have the courage to do it? And was she going to be able to, without falling to her death?

Gulping, but trying her best to quell the fear that surged inside her, Mary headed to the window, peering out at the dizzying view below.

It was far up. This was a tall castle, and her stomach twisted afresh as she thought about how sheer and high those walls looked from the outside. The window latch was rusty and it fought her attempts to open it until, after an arm-burning struggle, she finally wrenched the catch open.

Cold air streamed in as she opened it as wide as she could go and peered out, an action that caused her stomach to knot even tighter.

The biggest drawback was the window's height.

But once she got past the size of that intimidating drop, Mary began seeing the positives.

Firstly, the window looked out over an isolated part of the castle. A barren stretch of lawn, with fields beyond, was her only view. So she wouldn't be seen.

And the second positive – it was difficult to hunt for them in a situation so bleak, but Mary firmly encouraged herself to do it – was that the window was surrounded by a gnarled, tough looking creeper. It wound its way up the walls, and while it did look thorny, it also looked solid.

If she could get out of that window – if she could find a handhold and a foothold to start her off – then perhaps she might be able to scramble down without killing herself.

Taking a deep breath and gingerly stretching her leg over the sill, Mary embarked on her death-defying downward climb.

CHAPTER TWENTY FIVE

Once her leg was in place, lodged in a gnarled, leafy fork, Mary tested the creeper for strength. She wanted to do that before she committed all her weight to it. She had visions of the creeper peeling off the wall and arching out and sending herself plummeting to the ground below.

Those visions were not what she wanted in her mind at such a time, and Mary did her best to banish them.

The creeper seemed tough enough, so she put her full weight on the branch, and then, moving out, got a handhold.

With feet and hands now on the creeper, clutching it like a very large and terrified squirrel, Mary then began the difficult job of lowering herself down.

Step by step, looking for footholds and handholds as she went, she edged her way down. Her heart was firmly lodged in her throat, and her brain was screaming at her that this was a terrible, mad, dangerous idea, but luckily her hands and feet were cooperating enough to keep her going.

"At least," she panted, looking for a positive yet again, "I'm heading down. Getting closer to the ground with every step, right?"

But the ground was still a long way away, and sections of this creeper were frighteningly slippery. Slick with damp, and smooth from years of being scoured by the elements, on two occasions her foot slid so badly that she lost her foothold completely, and had to thrash around for purchase, while clinging on for grim death by her hands.

As she went, she managed to work out the best technique for survival, and descent, of this precarious ladder to freedom. If she wedged her feet into a fork of the creeper so that they were firmly lodged there, it seemed to work well. The only drawback was that it was difficult to dislodge her feet once wedged there. She had to tug them out, and one particularly hard tug nearly claimed her shoe. It was only by scrunching up her toes and hastily pushing her foot in place, that Mary didn't lose it completely.

The other necessity was to avoid the thorns – where possible. They were occasional, but long and sharp, and when her dress got stuck on them, she had to wiggle free, because there were no hands and feet to spare, to disentangle her.

This truly was fraught with peril! Despite her best efforts, there were a few occasions where the thorns ripped a great hole in her skirt or her bodice. There were a few rips in her uniform by the time she was at the second floor window, that she feared might be beyond the powers of a darning needle to fix.

She'd hoped that she could get in that window, and not have to continue with her climb, but her hopes were dashed when she saw this was the library window – and two people were in there, seated in chairs. She could see the backs of their heads, and she had an idea that one might be Duchess Drakeley.

At least they were facing the fire, not the window! But even so, her heart sped up even faster as she negotiated that tricky section of creeper. One wrong move now, one misstep – even one piece of bad luck, with Duchess Drakeley glancing up as she sensed a shadow over the window – and this could all be over.

She was about four yards up when, out of the corner of her eye, she saw she was no longer alone.

Somebody was standing at the bottom of the creeper, dressed in a waterproof jacket and a tweed cap, and as her panicked glance took in his presence, Mary got such a fright she lost her footing again.

This time, it was bad. Both feet were flailing around in the empty air, and worse still, a handhold had slipped. It was only the strength of her left hand, clutching the creeper with all her might, that was saving her.

Then, a voice came from below.

"Mary! Hang on, Mary! I'm coming!"

It was Gilbert!

She'd thought him gone. He was still there? And now, he was leaping for the creeper himself. It swayed and rustled as he clambered hastily up. Her arm was burning, but she refused to let go. She clamped her fingers in place – and then, she felt his hand close around her right ankle. The fingers were warm and firm.

"I've got you. Here's a foothold," he said, breathlessly.

His hand guided her foot to a sturdy fork in the creeper, and she put her weight on it with a gasp of thankfulness. Now, she could look for another handhold, and lower herself down again. He was climbing too, staying below her, the creeper managing to take both their weight.

And then, he was down and grasping her by the waist as she completed her pulse-pounding journey. But her pulse wasn't pounding any less as she touched down on solid ground, with Gilbert's hands still clasping her.

She turned around to face him. He looked utterly shocked and as scared as she'd been.

"I thought you'd gone home," she said.

"I wouldn't have gone without finding you and saying goodbye!" he protested. "I'm not going anywhere until this is solved, and I know you're going to be alright. And not defying gravity by clambering down the side of the castle wall," he added in heartfelt tones.

"It was, unfortunately, necessary," she said. "I'm glad you were nearby, though."

"I was out for a walk to clear my head and get some time to myself. I was all the way on the edge of the field." He was breathing hard, practically panting. "I saw you climb out of the window and – well, I ran here! As fast as I could!" Staring at her incredulously, he asked, "What's up? Were you locked in that room?"

Unfortunately, Gilbert had guessed right, and now, she had to admit to the truth. There was no way she could tell him an untruth or give him anything other than the correct facts. After all, there was an element of doubt in his mind about her now.

Gilbert would have to take sides, and decide whether he was prepared to believe her, or whether he was going to hand her over to the police.

"I was locked in there by Constable Philpott," she said.

His face tautened into a mask of concern. "But Mary, I –"

"I'm not guilty," she said. She was realizing that his hands were still clasped around her waist, while they were talking. It was very strange to be having this conversation, while in such close proximity to him. She wondered if he even realized he was still holding her. Well, she wasn't about to tell him, in case he stopped.

"I'm not guilty, but the constable hasn't yet found anyone else who is," she said. "He still has more people to question, but he didn't like it that I was interfering. I think the Drakeleys are convinced I am guilty, and so he decided the best thing was to keep me out of the way."

That was the most she could say. She didn't want to tell him that the constable's own suspicions of Mary were multiplying with every hour that passed, and every other suspect who was cleared. She personally didn't think Philpott's police training school had been very good, and to her, there had been a distinct lack of emphasis in the curriculum on good, hard questioning.

But that was just a theory, and she couldn't waste time wishing things had been different.

"Why didn't you stay in the study? Surely he'll find the killer soon?"

Mary shook her head.

"I have a theory," she told him. "I think I know who it is, and it's nobody that Philpott would suspect."

"And who's that?" Gilbert asked curiously, but Mary shook her head. She was going to keep her theory to herself, until she could actually find the elusive valet.

"If it works out, then there'll be an arrest shortly," she said. "If I can prove his guilt, I know Constable Philpott will be able to see it, too. But I need to do it before he – before the constable gives up on questioning people, and thinks it has to be me after all," she ended uneasily.

Gilbert nodded. Finally, his hands let go of her waist and he stepped back. He took a deep breath. Watching his face, Mary knew this was the deciding moment. Gilbert was picking sides.

"I trust you," he said eventually. "You found the killer the last time this happened. I want you to stay out of danger, though." Again, he glanced up at the castle wall, clearly wondering whether this would even be a possibility with Mary's talent for getting into sticky situations.

"I'll do my best to stay out of all trouble," she said.

"I wish I could help," he said. "But as a guest, in these circumstances, I think perhaps the best thing I can do is stay with the Drakeleys, and try to open their minds again to other possibilities."

"Diana's on my side," she reassured him. "Between you both hopefully you can have an effect, and stop them from calling for my arrest. And now, I'd better go."

"Good luck," he said.

It took an effort of will to turn away from him, and hurry around the side of the castle, leaving Gilbert behind. But hopefully, before too long, they'd be able to have another conversation in easier circumstances. All she needed to do was find the killer.

And her first stop was going to be Hugh Barnsby-Loxton's room. She remembered how Beamish had officiously shooed her and Hannah out, as soon as he arrived on the scene. Even then, she now realized he'd been managing the situation and trying to make sure he had sol control over his employer's interactions and activities. He must have been patiently waiting for the chance to administer that poison, and when it arrived, he seized it.

Mary trod quietly up the stairs, going along the corridor to the room where, just a couple of short days ago, she'd started unpacking Hugh's possessions without a care in the world.

Now she felt crushed by care and worry. This The stakes could not be higher. Mary could not afford to wonder what would happen if she couldn't trick Mr. Beamish into confessing – or worse still, if she was wrong.

She couldn't be wrong, she reminded herself. Beamish had the means, motive and opportunity to commit this clearly preplanned crime.

And he was here!

As she approached, she could hear the sound of singing from inside. It was the sound of Greensleeves, tunelessly rendered. And as well as humming, Beamish was chatting away to himself while he worked. His voice was clearly audible through the partially open door.

Imagine if he said something incriminating right now, believing he'd gotten away free and clear with the crime?

Stepping closer, Mary listened carefully, hoping that this would give her an all-important insight into his mind.

CHAPTER TWENTY SIX

"Alas my love, you dooo me wrooong," Beamish warbled, his discordant tone causing Mary to wince. Then, abandoning his song, the valet sighed. Mary listened carefully as he muttered to himself.

"Now, who was where, earlier on, and who could have done this? It couldn't be the maid, she had no reason to kill him, she was just about the only one he never spoke harshly to. It could surely not have been the lord or lady, they wanted him alive. I wonder… For I have loooved you well and looong… That must be it! Maybe I should go there!"

There was a thump and a scuffle from inside the room, and just in time, Mary leaped through the opposite door, which led to a linen closet, and flattened herself against the wall.

Beamish headed purposefully out, and he was so intent on where he was going, he didn't even glance in her direction. But Mary's mind was racing with ideas.

Perhaps Beamish was simply curious, and playing the role of an amateur sleuth instead of a valet? But it was surely also possible, and even more likely, that Beamish had committed this crime, and was now busy identifying a suspect that he could point fingers at, to make sure he was cleared of suspicion.

Either way, she needed to follow him, and learn what he knew. Where was he heading, and what was he hoping to find?

If he framed someone other than her, who ended up being accused of the crime, that would be terrible. And with Constable Philpott's talent for not observing the finer details or asking the right questions, it was all too possible.

Mary knew what it was like to be wrongfully accused. There was no worse feeling in the world. Imagine if he succeeded, and if somebody innocent ended up facing life imprisonment, or worse, for a crime they hadn't committed?

She had to follow him. If she caught him in the act of planting evidence, it might prove his guilt.

Tiptoeing out of the linen closet, and wishing she wasn't having to go to such reckless lengths in order to clear herself and everyone else, she walked soundlessly after him.

It was surprisingly difficult to keep up, because Beamish's pace was purposeful and he was weaving his way through the corridors erratically, taking a route that she soon guessed was chosen to keep him out of other people's sight.

That was lucky for her. She did not want to be in anyone's sights at the moment, but it made her even more certain that he was the killer, and that this pursuit could turn deadly in a moment.

And then, as he ascended a staircase, she realized where he was going.

Diana's room!

Did he suspect her? Or was he looking to frame her? This was horrific. Diana had tried her best to protect Mary, and now it was time for her to do the same. Mary knew full well that Diana couldn't be the killer, but if evidence was planted, or things were made to look that way, it might be enough to convince Constable Philpott.

Unerringly, Beamish entered Diana's room, pausing only for a moment to listen outside. Then, he pushed the door open and disappeared in, as swift and silently as a rat might wriggle through a gap in the stones.

From inside the room, Mary heard his breathing, and the sound of doors being opened. He wasn't humming any longer, or talking to himself. He was working in hasty silence, and she worried that he might be planting a piece of evidence that she wouldn't find. Hidden evidence, which he'd disclose at the crucial moment and which would take Diana down.

No time to waste. She had to act.

Taking a deep breath, Mary stepped into the room, turned, and closed the door quietly. That small sound was enough to alert Beamish, who at that moment was rummaging around on the bottom shelf of Diana's wardrobe.

With a surprised grunt, he tried to stand up, hit his head on the top shelf, and reeled back, clutching it in his hands. Gasping in pain, he whirled around to stare at her.

She returned his gaze, taking in his frantic demeanor, his tense pose, and the smear of dust on the shoulder of his dark valet's suit that she guessed meant this wasn't the first place he'd been rooting around in.

"What are you doing here?" he asked in a shaking voice.

"That's not the right question!" Outrage surged inside her. "What are *you* doing here? You left your room and came here via a circuitous route. Why?"

His jaw jutted. This valet was not going down without a fight.

"You followed me out of my room and came here behind me, on the same circuitous route, and perhaps I should be asking you that question, Miss Adams!"

"You were hoping to frame Diana!"

"You were hoping to frame *me*!" he retorted, leaving Mary briefly at a loss for words.

"I was doing no such thing," she replied.

"Nor was I." His voice was defensive, but the truth was that if she didn't break this cycle of conversation, they were going to end up accusing each other of things, and denying them, until somebody walked in and found them here.

"Alright," she said. "Why did you come here?" That was better. That was an open question, rather than an accusing one. That gave him the chance to explain himself. Mary realized that investigation was certainly a skill you learned as you went along, even though she had never wanted the lesson.

"I had a sudden thought," he said. "I've been thinking very hard about who could have done this, because I want to find the right killer." His jaw clenched and she saw real anger in his eyes. "Whoever it is deserves to go down for this crime, and I'm not convinced it's you!"

Mary's mind was spinning.

"You don't think it's me?"

"You don't have a reason to kill my employer. Others do. Most particularly, Miss Drakeley, Duchess-to-be. I know she sensed that my employer wanted the title more than he wanted her, and I do believe that she might have been aware of his very unfortunate indiscretions, while here." He sighed. "I did advise him he should refrain from doing anything while here, but it was sometimes hard to tell Mr. Barnsby-Loxton what to do. In fact, it was impossible."

"So you were planting evidence here?" Mary was still battling to follow the speedy twists that events were taking.

"I was looking for evidence!" With his hands on his hips, he glared at her crossly. "How many times do I have to tell you that I'm trying to find the killer?" Even though his voice was furious, he kept his tone low.

And so did she, when she replied.

115

"But – but why would you do that? I mean, why are you so strongly motivated?"

That, Mary thought, was a better approach than to keep telling him he was the killer himself. He stopped listening to her immediately when she did that. If he was, then she was going to need to find another way of getting there.

"I am furious that he died," Beamish said, surprising her.

"He didn't treat you well. I heard him being rude to you. He treated all servants badly, including you. And you could easily have found another job. I mean, you seem… efficient enough?" she said, doubtfully.

"Why thank you," he said, clearly offended by her faint praise. "You're right. I could have found another job, and I was going to. I never travel without receiving several offers of employment. I stayed with Mr. Barnsby-Loxton for a reason."

"What was the reason?"

"My employment with him was due to end on the day of his marriage. And on that day, there was a very generous severance package awaiting me. I was looking forward to it. It would have allowed me to take a month's holiday in the South of France, as well as bought some new clothes, and I've always wanted to have a long seaside holiday, while not at somebody's beck and call," he added sourly.

"So you were holding out for the severance package?" Light was dawning.

"I was. And now, I'm not getting it, because he can't be married if he's dead. So I'm furious, and feel that whoever has deprived me of it, deserves the consequences."

Mary was finally understanding Beamish's motives. It all made sense. He had stayed with Hugh because of the promised bonus, and now that it wasn't materializing, he was angry.

Of course, that ruled him out as the killer. There was every reason for him to have wanted Hugh alive and healthy until his wedding day.

"What a blow this has been," Beamish grumbled. "The only thing that'll set my mind at rest is if that miscreant is jailed for life. My bonus." He sighed, rubbing his head again.

"We'd better leave," Mary said. "Somebody might find us here. By the way, is there anyone… anyone you've ruled out so far?" She didn't know if Beamish would be willing to collaborate with her after their discussion had got off to such a bad start. But he shook his head.

"I was theorizing as I packed up. This was my first idea." He stared at her distrustfully. "Are you sure it's not right?"

"I'm sure. Diana had other plans. She was going to call off the engagement. She was waiting until after the announcement because – er…" It felt disloyal to speak about Diana's motives, but luckily Beamish had already figured it out.

"Oh, it's to do with that whole transfer of land, isn't it? She wanted the first hundred acres. Well, can't say I blame her for waiting until that came her way," he said. "But yes, if she was going to call it off, then it can't be her, and I've no idea who it could be. But I have help."

"You do?" Mary asked.

"I'm not the only one looking for evidence. Cameron Pratt is also searching. He told me he's convinced it was one of the servants, due to their oversensitivity to Hugh's bossy behavior, as he put it." While he said that, he had his valet's face on – an expressionless mask. Mary didn't much like Beamish – although she understood him a bit better now than she had done – but that poker face he was able to summon up, was something to admire.

"I'll carry on thinking."

But he said it in a final way, as if he'd picked sides, and anything he discovered would be shared with Cameron, and not with Mary. Clearly the discussion was over.

Mary watched as, still massaging his head tenderly, he marched out.

She followed, taking a circuitous route away from the bedrooms feeling discouraged and confused. This could not have gone worse Beamish did have a strong motive for wanting to keep Hugh in good health until the wedding. Money was a great persuader. That bonus, and the holiday in the South of France, had been enough motivation for him to put up with his employer's rudeness.

Now, she was all the way back where she started. Who was possibly left, who could have done this? She had no idea which direction to go in.

Only one possible way forward.

She needed to speak to Hannah urgently.

With time running out, and Constable Philpott closing in, perhaps her friend would have some ideas that could save the situation.

CHAPTER TWENTY SEVEN

"Hannah!" Mary whispered. After a hair-raising, stop-start foray through the castle, where she'd almost bumped into Constable Philpott once, and Duchess Drakeley twice, she'd finally tracked down her friend in the wine tasting room, which adjoined the small dining room.

Duster in hand, Hannah spun around, Mary's tone clearly triggering her anxiety.

"Is anything wrong? You sound like something is wrong," she said.

"Things couldn't be more disastrous," Mary admitted. "Constable Philpott accused me of investigating!"

"Oh, no!" Consternation and guilt warred for supremacy in Hannah's expression. "Did he tell you to stop?"

"He did worse than that," Mary said. Hannah clutched her feather duster in both hands, anxiously, as Mary elaborated. "He locked me in the small study, and I escaped through the window, climbing down a creeper."

Now, Hannah looked utterly horrified, eyes and mouth wide, as Mary continued.

"Worst of all, the suspect I escaped to find, because I was sure he was guilty, is cleared."

"Who was he?"

"Hugh's valet. But Beamish told me he would never have killed him, because he was getting a large bonus when his employment ended, on the day of the planned wedding."

"He would never have killed him if he had a bonus due. Who'd do that?" Hannah nodded her head.

"Beamish was looking for evidence. Apparently Cameron, Hugh's friend, is also looking for evidence and believes it's one of the servants. Everyone's trying to find this out."

"I wonder why Cameron would think it was one of the servants," Hannah said in a puzzled tone. "He's never had any difficulties with the staff, or any clashes. Hugh was the one who was rude, and demanding, and who you could never get a word in edgeways with, and had to stand and wait for ages because he was finishing off his story of singlehandedly rescuing the entire Allied forces during his Normandy operation."

"Hannah, we have to work out who it could be! Otherwise, Constable Philpott is going to end up arresting me, just because there's nobody else on his list."

"It's a real problem." Hannah scratched her head thoughtfully. "One of the staff? I wonder why Cameron thinks that? Is there something I've missed? I really can't see that any of them would be guilty, but what if I've overlooked something?"

Wide-eyed, she looked at her wits' end, which was exactly how Mary felt. How could this impossible crime have happened? Somebody had committed this murder, Hugh hadn't poisoned himself!

It also couldn't have been a mistake that he died, because he hadn't drunk soup made for anyone else. He was the only person at the table who'd ordered the cream of celery soup, which all the guests had eaten for lunch the previous day before the leftovers were returned to the cold room.

None of the other guests had been sick, none had died, none had choked to death.

And where had this poison even come from?

Mary shook her head. This wine tasting room was beginning to feel more like a trap than a refuge. She needed to go out and look for evidence – but what could she find, and how was she going to avoid detection by Constable Philpott. Her absence from the small study might be discovered at any moment, and then, she knew, her guilt would seem like a certainty.

The only thing that could have saved her was if she'd found the killer.

"The housekeeper, Miss Hobbs? Would she have done such a thing? The cook?" Hannah hazarded, but Mary could see from her face she was just clutching at straws, and didn't have any real reason for suspecting either of them.

Then, something even worse happened.

From down the passage came the frantic running of feet.

With their nerves already on edge, both Mary and Hannah spun around and faced the door.

It was Gilbert.

He burst into the room, his face taut with tension.

"Mary!" he gasped. "There you are. A terrible thing has happened."

"What? What's happened?" Mary's voice was quivering. She'd never known Gilbert to exaggerate, and now he looked stressed to the nines.

"I've been – looking for you – for the past ten minutes," he gasped. "I heard Constable Philpott… talking to Duchess Drakeley. He said that… the soup dregs were tested and contained traces of hemlock. And then, a poison vial was found in the castle – containing similar traces."

"A poison vial? Where?"

"Under your pillow!" Gilbert offered the bombshell as Mary drew in a horrified breath.

"Someone put it there." Her lips felt numb, and her voice didn't seem to belong to her at all. "Gilbert, it wasn't me. After everything that's happened… I would never lie to you. I didn't do it!"

"I know," Gilbert said. "Mary, you'd never have done such a thing. And if you had, I know you're far too clever to have hidden anything incriminating under your pillow. It was planted there – but Constable Philpott is now on the hunt for you. He's taking you straight in and accusing you of the crime. It's sheer luck that I found you first. I knew I had to warn you – but I'm not sure what we can do!"

Mary stared at him, into his troubled, deep blue eyes. She turned to look at Hannah, seeing her friend was clutching her apron tightly and tugging at the ruffles, a habitual action she often did when things were stressful.

This was all the way down to the wire. There was no more time left – but even as Mary's mind raced desperately ahead, she found herself surprisingly capable of clear thought. At last, the pieces she had been looking for were falling into place – and Beamish had provided the final and most crucial piece she needed.

This killer had planted evidence in her room to frame her. But by doing this, he had unwittingly revealed who he was.

"I think I've found the answer," she said. "And here's what we need to do. We must set a trap – and if we can do this, then the killer might walk straight in."

"But who is the killer? Have you worked it out? And what's the trap?" Hannah asked, while Gilbert glanced worriedly at the door.

"Yes," Mary said. "Planting that poison was a big mistake. I've worked out who he is at last."

She had only the sketchy makings of an idea to catch this man, and no time for any more detail. She didn't even want to reveal her suspicions to Hannah or Gilbert. Anything, right now, might alert the killer and result in him taking evasive action.

Taking a deep breath, she began to set out the plan that she hoped against hope might save her.

CHAPTER TWENTY EIGHT

Mary waited, side by side with Hannah, crouched in the most out-of-the-way hiding place she could think of. They were in the castle's dungeons themselves. The dungeons were all the way at the bottom of the west wing, and they were much more threatening in name than they were in actual physical reality.

At the end of a long, stone corridor, they were no more than three, low roofed, stone buildings with sturdy grilles in the side of the wall, through which a breath of cold air and light trickled.

The steel gates that must have held the prisoners inside were long gone, and the stonework was mossy and chipped. They were so far from anywhere, and so pervaded with damp, that most people had forgotten they existed.

There was a poetic justice, she thought, in the fact that they were hiding in an old dungeon, while hoping to avoid being in a new, modern one. They were perched on a piece of crumbling stone that must once have been the interleading wall between two cells. Now, it made a very uncomfortable and icy cold bench, but at least they didn't have to sit on the floor, which was wet and slick with damp.

"I wonder if Gilbert found Diana," Mary whispered. The plan hinged on him doing that, as fast as possible.

"I wonder if Diana managed to do what we needed her to do," Hannah whispered back.

It was so cold down here their breath was misting in the air, and it was dark and shadowy and forbidding. Scuttling noises from the shadows surrounding them made Mary turn her head in alarm.

A mouse, she didn't mind, but a rat would be scary, and a spider more terrifying still. And no matter what creatures poked their heads out of the gaps in the stonework, Mary knew that she and Hannah could not afford to utter a sound.

Everything hinged on Constable Philpott not finding them until the first part of the plan had been put into action.

It might not happen, too many guests might already have left, and Duke and Duchess Drakeley might not agree to it. But Mary didn't think the murderer would have left. Because the murderer wanted to see her arrested. Only then would he know his plan had worked, and that he would get off scot free after doing this terrible deed.

"Are you sure you know who it is?" Hannah brathed.

"I'm sure," Mary said.

"And how are you going to trap him?"

"I hope I'll be able to find a way."

"Is there any evidence that links him to the crime, do you know?" Hannah asked worriedly.

Mary swallowed. There was no direct evidence.

"I'm hoping that he'll reveal that himself," she said. This killer had covered his tracks with care and cunning, and this was going to take a good dollop of luck, along with the timing, and the element of surprise, that she hoped might swing the balance.

"How much longer is this going to take? I'm worried something's gone wrong," Hannah said. "Should I go up and take a look?"

"No," Mary cautioned her, speaking as softly as she could. "Sit tight. We need to stay here, and we can't risk being noticed by Constable Philpott until everything's ready upstairs. If he even gets a sniff of an idea we're down here, it'll be too late, and I'll be taken off to prison before we've had a chance to put these plans in place."

"This waiting's terrible. It's working on my nerves," Hannah admitted.

"Mine, too," Mary said.

"If something's gone wrong, what's our next plan?"

"Our next plan is to tell Constable Philpott when I'm at the police station. But I don't like that plan," Mary said.

Hannah shook her head. "Nor do I. I don't like it at all. I think our only chance is to get this right, because by the time he's got you in the handcuffs, he won't want to listen to anything."

That was a scary thought.

And, as they sat there in the semi-darkness, they heard footsteps approaching.

Mary's heart jumped all the way out of her mouth. This was either going to mean the start of their plan, or else, the end of it. It all depended on who was coming their way.

"Mary!"

It was Gilbert's voice. She jumped up from the hiding place. With Hannah close behind, she skedaddled to the door.

"Come quick! It took longer than we expected. Everyone was so scattered around." Gilbert quickly updated her as they hustled back along the narrow stone passage. "Diana did a great job. She rushed from place to place, looking excited and gleeful and telling everybody that they needed to gather in the parlor, now, because she was going to make a huge announcement. Her parents are there, but they don't look happy. The head butler and housekeeper, who got there early, are starting to get restless and need to leave, and some of the guests are making noises about departing."

"Is Constable Philpott there?"

"He wasn't when I left."

"Well," Mary said darkly, "if he hasn't already followed the crowds in that direction, I'm sure he will be there in no time, when he hears that I've joined the party."

They raced up the stairs, Mary taking them two at a time, noticing that a nasty cold draft was working its way through a large rip in her skirt. That had been from the thorns while climbing down the castle wall, and it felt like a lifetime ago. It said a lot for the speed of events that there hadn't even been time to change her skirt. She'd just have to appear before the assembled party in a tattered and torn state.

They rushed along the corridor, their three sets of rapid footsteps echoing off the walls. And then, there was the parlor ahead. This was the time of reckoning – and only now, in the next few minutes, would she know if her plan had succeeded.

Now, it was time for the first part of the plan to swing into action.

Mary headed on alone, with Gilbert and Hannah hanging back deliberately, so it wouldn't look like they were arriving as a group.

She burst into the parlor, then turned and looked at the assembled throng, letting shock and surprise show on her face. Diana half-sprang to her feet, fake consternation in her eyes.

"I'm – I'm sorry," Mary muttered. "I didn't know you were all in here."

She turned as if to leave, but consternation erupted among the guests. Duke Drakeley sprang to his feet.

"You're not going anywhere, young lady! You're suspected of a very serious crime!" His voice rang out as he made a beeline for the door, nearly colliding with Gilbert.

"Oh, sorry," both of them said.

"I thought I saw Miss Adams," Gilbert said, acting innocent, as if he'd also been on the lookout for her. "Oh, there she is! Should I call the police?"

The rest of the assembled throng had turned to watch this drama play out, their heads swinging back and forth as they followed the interaction. Mary saw, out of the corner of her eye, that Hannah had just sidled in through the opposite door and was standing quietly in a corner, surveying the scene.

"Call the police immediately!" Duke Drakeley ordered, his tone firm and commanding. "There's no doubt in my mind, thanks to the evidence, that Miss Adams is guilty. She should have been in prison a long time ago, and the sooner she's taken there, the better."

Nods from round about the parlor showed Mary that his sentiment was widely shared. Her stomach clenched. She hoped that this situation wasn't too far gone.

"I'll go and get Constable Philpott immediately. I'm sure he's searching the rooms for her after she escaped from the small study," Gilbert said.

But, as he turned back to the door, implacable footsteps sounded outside the entrance that Hannah had so recently used.

"No need to call me."

At a hurried walk, the constable entered. He looked somewhat puffed, and his face was redder than Mary remembered it being. She guessed that the pressure to find her had led to an accelerated search of the premises. At least, looking on the bright side, the constable didn't look cold. In fact, as he hurried in, he lifted his hat briefly off his head, as if hoping to draw some cooler air in, before replacing it, and focusing on her.

"Miss Adams, you are under arrest!" Determinedly, notebook at the ready, he advanced. "You have committed a heinous crime, and worse still, you have endeavored to conceal your guilt."

"Now, that's an announcement I'm glad to hear," Duchess Drakeley said, and applause rang out around the room. But Mary stood her ground. And, as Constable Philpott reached out his hand, clearly intending for her to offer her wrist for the handcuffs he was holding, Mary put her hands behind her back.

"Before you arrest me," she said, "you might want to hear what I have to say."

"Wait a minute!" Duke Drakeley blustered. "What's going on here? We all came into the parlor to hear an announcement that my daughter said she wanted to make. Not only have we not heard it, and we've been sitting here for several minutes now, but you've gone and stolen her thunder!"

"Unacceptable!"

"Terrible rude!"

"Definitely not cricket!"

The grumbles and complaints resounded, in upper-class tones, from the assembled guests. The servants, of course, stayed quiet – apart from Beamish the valet who added a low grumble to the general outpouring. But Mary noticed that the stranger, Lucas Everington, who also formed part of the throng, was not uttering any words of complaint, but was watching with a very intent expression on his face.

Now, on cue, Diana stood.

"I don't mind at all if Mary speaks," she said quietly. "My announcement can wait. I've always felt that Mary is innocent of what she's been blamed for. Maybe she would like a chance to explain herself."

"To confess, more likely," Cameron said, and a couple of the other ladies tittered.

"She deserves to rot in prison after murdering our son!" Mrs. Barnsby-Loxton said in sharp, furious tones. "All our other boys have married well and gained titles. Hugh would have done the same, and gained the best title of all, thanks to our very pleasing arrangement, if it were not for that maid's interference!"

Her husband rumbled out his agreement.

For a moment, Constable Philpott's resolute expression intensified. He jangled the cuffs thoughtfully, and Mary felt a flash of fear that despite Diana's agreement, she wouldn't get her wish, and the constable would cart her straight off to the cells.

But then, in easy and reasonable tones, Gilbert said, "It would be interesting to hear what she has to say, and with all of us here, there's no danger of her escaping. I'll stand by the door."

He strode over to stand squarely in the open doorway.

"And I'll stand by the other door!" Hannah squeaked, moving a few paces to her left and drawing herself up, puffing her chest out, trying to look bigger and more solid than she actually was.

The constable nodded, and made a 'go ahead', gesture to Mary.

"Alright," Duchess Drakeley said, officiously adding her permission to the proceedings. "But make it quick. I really came here to listen to my daughter, not to you."

"I'll be as quick as I can," Mary said.

It felt intimidating to be speaking in front of a crowd that was mostly swayed against her. She knew that it would take luck and timing to get further.

"I did not commit this crime," she said.

"Oh, this is ridiculous!" Mr. Barnsby-Loxton's voice rang out, sharp and angry. "I didn't come here to listen to lies! Officer, I demand that you arrest her now and take her away."

Mary could have told him that was a bad idea.

Constable Philpott stepped forward, glowering at Mr. Barnsby-Loxton. "Sir, as a highly trained officer of the law, I will do as I see fit. Right now, we're letting this young lady speak."

Once again, Mary began.

"I did not commit this crime," she said. She could see most of the guests were red-faced with the effort of wanting to shout her down, but they were keeping quiet for now. "You see," she continued, "I've been thinking about two things. Firstly, who would do this, and secondly, why. With everything that's been going on, and the engagement announcement, it's easy to forget that this crime was preplanned. Somebody sourced the poison – hemlock is readily available in the wild if you know where to find it, I believe – and they brought it here with the intent to murder Mr. Barnsby-Loxton. This was not an opportunistic crime, but carefully preplanned, and then committed at a time when there would be many guests and servants around."

"And why?" Hugh's father jeered.

Calmly, Mary replied. "The reason is jealousy and resentment."

There was a hush as everyone took in the words. She gave a moment for this to sink in, before continuing. "Mr. Barnsby-Loxton was a heroic soldier, but his actions during the war turned into something that he exaggerated over time, emphasizing his role, until he had basically rewritten the story to imply that he alone was the reason his mission succeeded.

"Are you calling my son a liar?" Hugh's father threatened.

"Oh, hush!" Hugh's mother surprisingly said. "You know he did exaggerate that story, despite me telling him numerous times he shouldn't."

"It unfortunately proved to be a fatal decision," Mary said. "Because after listening over and over again to the story, there was one person who finally broke, and who decided they simply couldn't take hearing it one more time. That they couldn't deal with listening to Hugh act as if he had done this all on his own. Especially since the

127

other person involved had been injured during this heroic mission, while Hugh came out of it scot-free."

Mary lifted a hand and pointed.

"Cameron Pratt, you became more and more resentful of Hugh's story, and his need to take all the glory for himself. I think your jealousy must have reached a stage where it poisoned your mind. And you decided that, to stop that story from being told again, the answer was to poison your friend."

Her hand was shaking. She was so tense and so worried about this outcome. Pausing for breath, her mouth feeling dry, Mary realized that the room had fallen completely silent. Everyone was now looking from Mary, to Cameron, and back again.

"That's utter nonsense!" he said, but his voice was wobbling.

"Unfortunately, the evidence worked against you," Mary said, doing her best to sound as if there was no shred of doubt in her mind. "Because you told Beamish you were sure a servant had done it. You went on your own search of the servants' rooms."

She was briefly interrupted by Constable Philpott's furious snort.

"Is there any point in calling a detective to a murder scene when every guest in the manor house seems to think they can solve this crime?" he said angrily. "With all this interfering, it's a miracle any killer ever gets found, and let me tell you, country houses have a poor reputation in this regard. Respect the law, ladies and gentlemen!"

Mary continued, once the constable had finished having his moment of strong emotion.

"The evidence under my pillow was planted there by you, Cameron, while you pretended to search. You framed me for this murder, knowing that nobody would suspect you of killing your friend. If it hadn't been for Beamish, and for a comment you made to me earlier about the poison being from a plant, I would never have put two and two together. But you knew what the poison was before the soup was even tested. You told me so! You went and picked that hemlock, didn't you? You intended for your friend to die, all along. All that mattered was finding the right time!"

Throughout her explanation, Mary had been watching Cameron's face. As she spoke, it had been getting darker and darker, as if it had bypassed the stage of red, and gone straight on to purple. She hoped that her accusation had made him angry enough to blurt out a confession. Because now, the final part of her plan rested on Cameron losing his temper.

He stared straight at her. With a little smile, he said, "Brilliant imagination, my dear little maid. What a creative young lady you are. Unfortunately, the evidence is against you, and you might as well acknowledge that everything you've said is just hot air."

And she knew, with a chill, that he'd anticipated her plan. At this critical moment, her suspect was going to hold his nerve. And that might be the deciding factor he needed, that would swing the finger of guilt around to her again.

CHAPTER TWENTY NINE

She needed to taunt him! Right now, Mary knew, some urgent prodding was needed to tip the wily Cameron Pratt over the edge. But, as if sensing exactly what needed to be done, Hannah acted before Mary had even had the chance to open her mouth.

"I'm willing to speak for my friend," she said firmly. "Because what you don't know, Mr. Pratt, is that our bedclothes get changed on a weekly basis, and I'm responsible for our room. I stripped down the beds first thing this morning, and put fresh sheets and pillowcases on. There was no poison vial under that pillow."

That unexpected voice of support was clearly startling. Cameron Pratt swung around to glare at Hannah.

"You're lying!" he said. "What rot! You're standing up for your friend, and you should also go to prison for doing it!"

"Actually!" Another voice rang out from the other side of the room. This time it was the housekeeper, Miss Hobbs. She drew herself up, looking a little scared, but resolute. "Actually, Mr. Pratt, I can confirm that Hannah Jones changed the sheets in that room this morning. I'm sure she would have reported any poison to me – and might I add, it would be very strange for a killer who'd used such a substance, not to dispose of it immediately. The only reason I can think of for keeping it is to put it somewhere with the intention of it being found."

Mary felt weak with gratitude. The dear, brave housekeeper was speaking up in her defense, and doing so in very difficult circumstances. And no sooner had she finished speaking than Barbara, from the laundry room, spoke up.

"Those sheets arrived in my laundry room, from Basement Room Three, before Mary had even arrived to help with the washing. Hannah must have stripped the beds as soon as she got up."

"I passed by a little later," the cook admitted. "I looked in to see if I needed to leave Miss Adams any breakfast in her room. She was asked to take her meals there after all this occurred. And I can say, with certainty, that those sheets were new. I noticed the fold marks on them, you see. It's only the guests' beds that we smooth out with the iron to make sure they're flat. The servants' beds, as long as everything's clean and neat, we don't bother."

Mary felt breathless as she listened to servant after servant standing up, speaking out, supporting her in public, against the obnoxious friend of the man who'd treated every single servant appallingly. It wasn't often that servants got the chance for revenge. But now, Mary could see, they were taking it.

And as person after person spoke, Cameron Pratt was getting angrier and angrier. His face looked like it was about to burst into flames.

"You're all liars!" he shouted, his voice so loud and violent that the people standing near him startled at the sound, whirling around to face him. "You're all liars and covering for each other! Now lock her up!"

"And what's more likely?" Mary asked sweetly. "That we're all liars – or that there's only one liar in this room, and it's the person who also happens to be a killer?"

His chest rose and fell rapidly. His fists clenched. A vein in his forehead, that Mary had never seen before, was now pounding visibly.

"The damned man deserved it!" he roared. "That stupid story! I was the one who led the mission. I was the one who had to dole out the French bread and tinned ham that we lived on for a week! I was the one who mapped the route and planned the attack and organized our escape. Single handed?" Fury laced his voice as it rose to a scream. "The only reason I got a bullet in the leg was that stupid Hugh Barnsby-Loxton delayed our evacuation because he was flirting with a French peasant woman whose house we were using!"

Everyone was watching now. Everyone was listening as, at last, the new version of the story was told.

"Time after time, I had to listen to it. Time after time he changed it, and every time, I mattered less and did less, until I didn't exist in that story at all! Poisoning was too good for him! I should have thrown him out of a third-floor window and told him to enjoy the ride!"

The silence in the parlor was palpable. The only sound was Cameron's harsh breathing. And then, gradually, reason seemed to return to the impassioned man, and Mary watched his eyes widen as he realized what he'd said.

"Oh, no!" he muttered.

Spinning around, he plunged through the assembled guests, making for the far exit door.

"Hannah! Watch out!" Mary yelled. She didn't want her friend hurt!

But Cameron was in too much of a hurry to hurt anyone.

He simply grabbed hold of her shoulder and shoved her aside so that she collided hard with the butler.

And then, in a flurry of limbs, he was out of the door.

"Chase him down!" Gilbert yelled. "He's a guilty man! Chase him!"

First out of the door, with vengeance in his eyes, was none other than Beamish the valet. Beamish was closely followed by Duke Drakeley.

"You murdered my future son-in-law!" he yelled, a comment that Mary knew wasn't accurate, because Diana had been going to call off the engagement, but it was certainly heartfelt.

And third out of the door, with an amazing turn of speed, was Constable Philpott himself. Somehow, the long legged constable had managed to cross the parlor floor and erupt through the far door in a record time. He might not be the world's fastest thinker, Mary acknowledged, but the speed he showed in pursuing a suspect was awe-inspiring.

"You killed my son! Damn you! I always suspected you were two-faced, and not a real friend at all!" Hugh's father was hot on his heels, bursting out of the door with a wrathful cry.

And then, she was running, and so was Gilbert, and Hannah was joining the chase, after apologizing to the butler. The butler himself, in a portly and dignified way, was also setting off through that door. Diana, in her wobbly high heels, was teetering in pursuit. The housekeeper was following at a jog, and even Duchess Drakeley and Mrs. Barnsby-Loxton were bringing up the rear at a brisk though dignified walk, holding tightly to their hats.

Surely a man with a limp couldn't outrun them all, Mary thought.

She couldn't even see where he'd gone! All she could see, as she powered along the castle's narrow corridor, were the people ahead of her.

Everyone veered right down a side corridor, and she followed. Then everyone veered left, down the narrow passage that led to the library. And then, in an unexpected twist, she saw the people ahead of her all veer down the passage that led to the kitchen.

Through the kitchen they ran, in single file, twisting and turning between the weathered steel counters. Where was he heading? Was he going to race outside?

There was a commotion ahead, shouts and cries. People were skidding and sliding, and as Mary reached the back of the kitchen, she did the same, shrieking as she suddenly felt as if she was on an ice rink. Yelling and waving his arms, Beamish skidded across the floor until he ended up in an embrace with the stovepipe.

Cameron had poured oil on the floor! It was causing a terrible pile-up as the followers lost their footing. Landing on his backside in a pool of oil, Duke Drakeley was finding it impossible to rise, slipping and sliding as he tried to get to his feet again. Even Constable Philpott was navigating the floor like a drunken man, bent over and waving his arms.

Clutching at the counter for support, Mary stepped through and over and around the others, and gingerly slid and skidded her way through the oil.

But now, as they reached the scullery door and headed out into the courtyard and the firmer purchase of the rough tiles, people were scattering.

"Where is he?" somebody called.

"How could he have gotten away?" someone else shouted.

"Did he go down to the stables?" she heard Diana cry in a confused voice.

But Mary was wondering something different. Would he really have headed into the open, with that limp, and the lack of speed it brought? Would a cunning man have chosen that route? Had he gone through the kitchen at all – or had he doubled back?

She knew that kitchen well – and maybe, the sneaky Cameron Pratt had learned its layout too.

There was a big cupboard under that counter. A cupboard where all the largest vats of sugar and flour were kept, but in which there was always plenty of room for more.

Was he hiding there?

"Gilbert!" she shouted. "Constable Philpott! Maybe he is still inside?"

Some of the stragglers had given up on the chase because there were no more people coming through.

Seeing that both Gilbert and Constable Philpott were veering away and heading back in her direction, Mary returned to the scullery and rushed through the kitchen.

Reaching the slippery oil, which was now smeared with a multitude of footprints, this time, she slid onto her hands and knees and let herself glide along.

She slowed when she neared the cupboard and put out an oily hand to try to stop herself. It skidded on the painted door and almost slipped right off the handle.

But Mary managed to tug the handle, and peered into the dark recesses of that cupboard.

A pair of wide, startled eyes stared back.

"He's here!" She shouted the words in relief, knowing that Cameron's sneaky attempt to escape had failed, and that he was now, finally, cornered. "He's here!'

The next moment, Constable Philpott cannoned into her from behind, grasping at the edge of the cupboard to stop his progress. And beyond, slipping and sliding, but with grim determination on his face, Gilbert was fighting to stay on his feet as he headed toward them.

"Cameron Pratt," Constable Philpott said, breathlessly but firmly, staring into the cupboard on his hands and knees while, with some difficulty, he extricated the handcuffs from his belt again. And to Mary's deep relief, he finally uttered the words that cleared her at last. "Come out of there. You are under arrest for the murder of Hugh Barnsby-Loxton."

CHAPTER THIRTY

"Well, Mary Adams. You are clearly a highly intelligent and resourceful woman. The way in which you identified the killer, while clearing your own name, was – well, admirable, is a word I should use." Duchess Drakeley sounded calm and composed as she delivered her verdict.

It was evening, and everyone had managed to clean themselves up after the chase.

After the police had left, the Drakeleys had requested Mary's presence, in the parlor, as soon as she was in a fit state to be seen.

Heading swiftly down to the basement, Mary had had a bath in the small, shared bathroom, scrubbing the oil from her hands and legs, and had then dressed herself up in her clean, spare uniform.

Now, she was standing on the rug, with her cleanly scrubbed hands folded in front of her, facing Duke and Duchess Drakeley, who were seated side by side on the plush, though somewhat faded, two-seater sofa.

"Yes. Your agility of thinking was quite remarkable," Duke Drakeley added.

"Thank you," Mary said humbly, deciding that a response was in order, even though she had no idea where, exactly, this interview was headed.

"It is with regret," Duchess Drakeley then said, a word which made Mary's heart race with anxiety, "that we have to terminate your employment as a member of Castle Drakeley's household team. In recognition of your efforts, we will, of course, give you a month's severance pay."

"In fact," Duke Drakeley added, stroking his short beard, "I would go so far as to say a small bonus is in order, for exceptional performance, above and beyond the call of duty."

"Yes," his wife said decisively. "A bonus will be allocated to your final pay packet."

Mary stared from one to the other of them in consternation. She had no idea why they were doing this! It seemed like their words were at odds with their actions, and she could make no sense of it at all. This

135

was an outcome she'd never expected. In fact, it was akin to a disaster. Losing her third job in as many months? How was this possible?

"Might I ask," she ventured – deciding since she'd been dismissed anyway, it couldn't really make things worse. "Might I ask why? I've done my best and I – I solved the crime. I didn't cause it."

Duchess Drakeley shook her head. "It's got nothing to do with your work performance. You're one of our hardest workers ever. And it certainly has nothing to do with your resourcefulness in solving the crime."

"But then – why?" Mary pleaded, wondering if there was any way of redeeming the situation.

"It's your friendship with our daughter," Duchess Drakeley said.

"Diana? She's the reason you're doing this?"

Duke Drakeley continued as his wife folded her hands.

"Diana has always been a reckless spirit. And both of us feel that, at this house, you're a bad influence on her."

"After all, you told her to follow her heart and not to enter into a very satisfactory engagement," Duchess Drakeley added.

"But – but it wasn't satisfactory for her!" Mary said, appalled they were doing this. "And Hugh would have been murdered regardless. Nothing I did could have changed anything."

"It's not what you did – it's what you might do. Diana does not need somebody like you, encouraging her wayward spirit. Because of that, we have decided you are better off apart. She has announced to us she will marry Harold Burbridge, and while he is not a man we would have chosen, we hope that she will be happy, and that marriage will calm her down." Duchess Drakeley stared at Mary, now with a hint of apology in her eyes. "She is our only daughter. And we would like to see her on a more settled path." She paused. "I know you arrived here with your friend, Hannah. If she chooses to leave with you, we will offer her the same terms and the same bonus. She, however, is welcome to stay, as she's not led our daughter astray."

Mary sighed. These parents were simply impossible. She might be going to leave, but she wasn't going to abandon this friendship. She was going to make sure to stay in touch with Diana, whatever the future brought. Friends were friends, and no amount of parental interfering was going to change that.

However, there was no point in arguing. This situation was a fait accompli, and now she would have to look for a new job.

"Thank you," she said politely, leaving a lot of words unsaid.

She turned and walked out of the parlor. Despite her jobless predicament, she did feel a distinct sense of relief to be turning her back on the Drakeleys, and their controlling ways, forever.

Heading out into the corridor with a worried heart, she knew she'd need to find Hannah urgently and explain their predicament. Her friend had a choice to make, and tough though it was, Mary was going to encourage her to stay here and keep the steady job she had.

But, as she headed down the corridor, a figure stepped out of the library with abrupt suddenness – as if he'd been listening and waiting for her, she thought in surprise.

It was Lucas Everington, the mysterious stranger. And now, he was heading directly toward her, with an expectant look.

"Mary," he said. "I – well, I've been wanting to speak to you. It's quite urgent now, as I have to leave. I didn't realize things would get so complicated at these big country castles, and I've run out of excuses to stay here."

"You've been wanting to speak to me ever since you arrived," Mary said. "Isn't that right? You didn't have business with the Drakeley's at all, did you?"

He shifted from foot to foot, looking embarrassed. "Well, I wanted to – to observe you and to check your credentials, and to make sure you were who you said you were." He rubbed a hand over his buttery blond hair. "And then, with the murder and everything, the time wasn't right. But now that it's all solved…" He stared at her. "I'm family, Mary. I'm your second cousin on your mother's side. And ever since I got to hear of her death, I've been trying to find you."

CHAPTER THIRTY ONE

Family? The word was utterly shocking to Mary. She hadn't thought she had any family left in the whole world. Now, it felt as if her world had been turned upside down. She couldn't believe it! But it did make sense. Her mother had spoken of a sister who'd gone to France, and then lost touch, and then died of a fever.

And this man could be related to her. They even shared the same hair color. There was a family resemblance.

"I don't know what to say," she got out eventually. Her voice was shaking. "I've been feeling like I'm all alone in the world, and now I find I'm not? It's – well, it's a lot to take in. It's such a shock to know I have family!" Remembering her manners just in time, she added, "It was very kind of you to come and look for me."

"It's the least I could do." He added, in a quiet voice, "I've been – well, I've been lucky in my business dealings, and I've made a few good decisions along the way, and I've got a small business now where I renovate and sell manor houses and luxury homes. Not on the scale of this – smaller -but still on the high end of the market."

He took a breath. "I'm busy putting the finishing touches to a home now – it's a very lovely one, out in the countryside, near a scenic village about a hundred miles south of here. I was going to ask you if you'd like to come and stay for a few weeks – but when I saw how things were looking here, I changed my mind. I'd like to offer you a job for the next few months, while the renovations are complete. There are already tenants in the place who might end up buying it, so there'll be plenty to do. I can pay you a very good salary, and it'll be a chance to – well, to be with family again, because I'll be working just as hard on the house, and the gardens."

A job? She had a lifeline she'd never expected, coming from a direction that was still leaving her reeling.

Then, hurriedly, Lucas Everington continued.

"We are looking for other staff, too, and I understand you came here with your friend. So, if you'd both like to take the offer, then you're both welcome."

"This is not what I ever expected," Mary said. "I still can't believe it. But the offer is really kind, and it's come at the right time."

She knew now was not a moment for hesitation. "I'd like to accept on my behalf," she then told him. "And as for Hannah, I'm going to go straight downstairs and ask her. And – thank you again."

"It's the least I can do – for family," he said, with a wry, and surprisingly kind, smile.

Feeling as shocked as if the world had tipped her into a strange alternate universe she'd never known about, Mary headed downstairs to tell Hannah about the unexpected double shift in her fortune – and the discovery of her family.

EPILOGUE

"You're leaving?" Gilbert asked, and Mary nodded.

"I don't have a choice," she explained.

It was late in the evening, after dinner – a low key affair that was both an acknowledgment of the distressing events that had played out here, and a celebration of Diana's announcement that she and her true love would now be courting.

Mary felt thrilled for Diana and Harold. They had fought through adverse and unexpected circumstances to achieve this goal.

She hadn't served dinner, but she had been allowed to work behind the scenes, in the kitchens, under Mrs. Waddington's supervision. And straight after the meal, Gilbert had come to find her.

Now, they were standing out in that same pretty courtyard where she'd seen Lady Emily crying over Hugh.

"I've got to move on because I'm apparently a bad influence on Diana, according to her parents." She sighed. "At least Hannah is coming with me. That's something. She said yes immediately."

"I hope the surprise of finding out you have a distant family member, softened the blow," he said.

"The surprise of finding out I wasn't going to be arrested, that you didn't think I was a killer, and that I have surviving family in the world," she said, grinning at him. "Of them all, I can't decide which is the biggest relief."

"For me, they all are." It was dark out here, but she could see the flash of Gilbert's teeth as he smiled. "I think I would have had to go in and rescue you if they'd locked you up. Might have landed us both in trouble, but I'd have tried it regardless."

"And I'd have come with you if you'd filed through the bars," Mary said. It was true. After what they'd been through... she now trusted Gilbert. He was more than a friend. They'd been through way too much for this to stop at simple friendship.

"I'll miss you here," he said. "The Drakeleys are staid people, I know, but we'll be doing more business with them now that they've acquired more farmland and I'll be visiting regularly. But... where did you say Everington's manor house is located?"

"It's in Herefordshire, I believe," she said.

"Interesting. I have a few business opportunities down there, and I might be exploring them soon," he said.

"Oh, really? In that area?" Her heart skipped. The only drawback about accepting this offer had been the thought she wouldn't see Gilbert so often – if at all.

"If there weren't any business opportunities, I'd make some," he said firmly. "And if I couldn't make any, then I'd come down anyway. I want to see you again, Mary."

"And I want to see you again, Gilbert."

"Hopefully in better circumstances," he said, with a quirk of his eyebrow, that she saw, because the moon came out from behind a cloud at that moment, suffusing the courtyard in a faint, hazy glow.

"Don't take it as a certainty," she said. "Trouble seems to follow me around – or perhaps, I should say – it follows us around."

"I'll be ready for it."

He stepped forward, closer to her, and Mary felt her stomach flip-flop – but in a nice way, a happy way, unlike all the somersaults of fear and anxiety it had been doing throughout the past two days. This was something different.

Gilbert stroked her hair.

And then, he leaned forward, his hand cupping her face.

"Mary Adams. You're beautiful... and you're fascinating. And whatever trouble we get into in the future, I'm ready for it," he said gently.

Her heart accelerated. This was leading into uncharted territory, it was something she'd never expected, but something she'd always hoped for – even though she'd preferred adventure stories to romance novels. She'd always thought romance novels were a little disappointing and not exciting enough.

But, as Gilbert's lips touched hers, Mary realized with a flash of insight, that adventure and romance could be combined.

And that her life, and her friendship with him, would never be the same again.

NOW AVAILABLE!

THE MAID AND THE MANSION: AN UNSOLVABLE CRIME
(The Maid and the Mansion Cozy Mystery—Book 4)

In post-World War II England, a clever, young woman named Mary Adams finds herself thrust into a world of privilege and secrets as she transitions from being a wartime factory worker to a maid in the grand estates. In a stately ancestral home, a brewing family feud takes a deadly turn when a murder attempt on the heir, a young bachelor, goes awry. As tensions run high, Mary must navigate a treacherous landscape of family deception to unmask the killer before they can strike again....

"Very entertaining. I highly recommend this book to the permanent library of any reader that appreciates a very well written mystery, with some twists and an intelligent plot. You will not be disappointed. Excellent way to spend a cold weekend!"
--Books and Movie Reviews, Roberto Mattos (regarding *Murder in the Manor*)

THE MAID AND THE MANSION: AN UNSOLVABLE CRIME is book #4 in a charming historical cozy mystery series by Fiona Grace, #1 bestselling author of *Murder in the Manor*, which has over 10,000 five star reviews!

As Mary navigates the delicate intricacies of high society, she also finds herself privy to their darkest secrets. As a maid, Mary moves through mansions unnoticed and unheeded, allowing her to overhear tales of jilted lovers, gossip from fellow maids, and secrets straight from the mouths of the rich and elite.

As Mary delves deeper into the intricate web of secrets within the stately manor, she encounters a cast of eccentric and intriguing characters, each with their own secrets—and their own motives for murder.

Will Mary uncover their secrets in time? Or become just another story whispered about in the grand halls?

A charming historical cozy mystery series that transports readers back in time, THE MAID AND THE MANSION is mystery at its finest: spellbinding, atmospheric and impossible to put down. A page-turner packed with shocking twists, turns and a mystery that's hard to solve, it will leave you reading late into the night, all while you fall in love with its unforgettable heroine.

Future books in the series are now available!

"The story line wasn't just a who done it, but had a story about her life and romance, including village life. Very entertaining."
--Amazon reviewer (regarding *Murder in the Manor*)

"It has endearing and sometimes quirky characters, a plot that keeps you reading and the right amount of romance. I can't wait to start book two!"
--Amazon reviewer (regarding *Murder in the Manor*)

"What a great story of murder, romance, new beginnings, love, friend ships and a wonderful cascade of mystery."
--Amazon reviewer (regarding *Murder in the Manor*)

"This is a clean contemporary romance that you will find hard to put down!"
--Amazon reviewer (regarding *Always, Forever*)

"A bit of romance and a very determined woman! I have read many of Fiona Grace's novels and loved every one of them—this was no exception. I am looking forward to reading the rest of this new series!"
--Amazon reviewer (regarding *Always, With You*)

Fiona Grace

Fiona Grace is author of the LACEY DOYLE COZY MYSTERY series, comprising nine books; of the TUSCAN VINEYARD COZY MYSTERY series, comprising seven books; of the DUBIOUS WITCH COZY MYSTERY series, comprising three books; of the BEACHFRONT BAKERY COZY MYSTERY series, comprising six books; of the CATS AND DOGS COZY MYSTERY series, comprising nine books; of the ELIZA MONTAGU COZY MYSTERY series, comprising nine books (and counting); of the ENDLESS HARBOR ROMANTIC COMEDY series, comprising nine books (and counting); of the INN AT DUNE ISLAND ROMANTIC COMEDY series, comprising five books (and counting); of the INN BY THE SEA ROMANTIC COMEDY series, comprising five books (and counting); and of the MAID AND THE MANSION COZY MYSTERY series, comprising five books (and counting).

Fiona would love to hear from you, so please visit www.fionagraceauthor.com to receive free ebooks, hear the latest news, and stay in touch.

A SPEAKEASY DEMISE (Book #4)
A FLAPPER FATALITY (Book #5)
BUMPED BY A DAME (Book #6)
A DOLL'S DEBACLE (Book #7)
A FELLA'S RUIN (Book #8)
A GAL'S OFFING (Book #9)

LACEY DOYLE COZY MYSTERY
MURDER IN THE MANOR (Book#1)
DEATH AND A DOG (Book #2)
CRIME IN THE CAFE (Book #3)
VEXED ON A VISIT (Book #4)
KILLED WITH A KISS (Book #5)
PERISHED BY A PAINTING (Book #6)
SILENCED BY A SPELL (Book #7)
FRAMED BY A FORGERY (Book #8)
CATASTROPHE IN A CLOISTER (Book #9)

TUSCAN VINEYARD COZY MYSTERY
AGED FOR MURDER (Book #1)
AGED FOR DEATH (Book #2)
AGED FOR MAYHEM (Book #3)
AGED FOR SEDUCTION (Book #4)
AGED FOR VENGEANCE (Book #5)
AGED FOR ACRIMONY (Book #6)
AGED FOR MALICE (Book #7)

DUBIOUS WITCH COZY MYSTERY
SKEPTIC IN SALEM: AN EPISODE OF MURDER (Book #1)
SKEPTIC IN SALEM: AN EPISODE OF CRIME (Book #2)
SKEPTIC IN SALEM: AN EPISODE OF DEATH (Book #3)

BEACHFRONT BAKERY COZY MYSTERY
BEACHFRONT BAKERY: A KILLER CUPCAKE (Book #1)
BEACHFRONT BAKERY: A MURDEROUS MACARON (Book #2)
BEACHFRONT BAKERY: A PERILOUS CAKE POP (Book #3)
BEACHFRONT BAKERY: A DEADLY DANISH (Book #4)
BEACHFRONT BAKERY: A TREACHEROUS TART (Book #5)
BEACHFRONT BAKERY: A CALAMITOUS COOKIE (Book #6)

Made in the USA
Las Vegas, NV
29 April 2024

89320457R00090